The Little World of
Edith Endsley

A Novel
By

Edward Beardsley

iUniverse LLC
Bloomington

THE LITTLE WORLD OF EDITH ENDSLEY

iUniverse books may be ordered through booksellers or by contacting:

iUniverse
1663 Liberty Drive
Bloomington, IN 47403
www.iuniverse.com
1-800-Authors (1-800-288-4677)

ISBN: 978-1-4759-9941-9 (sc)
ISBN: 978-1-4759-9943-3 (hc)
ISBN: 978-1-4759-9942-6 (e)

Printed in the United States of America.

iUniverse rev. date: 07/31/2013

For

Mary Might

CONTENTS

ONE

I F YOU STOOD AT THE convergence of lines leading from Montreal, Cuba, Mexico, and Louisiana you might be confused about the country of your location. In fact, you'd be just off dead center of the United States.

The convergence of these imaginary geographical lines is a sector bounded by the towns of Bluffton, Portland, Chamois, and Morrison in the American state called Missouri ("Dwellers of the Big Muddy," the Missouri River).

These four are small towns almost in the shadow of the great city of St. Louis, nicknamed "Mound City" for earthwork mounds left by the Indians, sites of the famous/infamous Dred Scott cases of 1847 and 1850 and of the birthplace of T.S. Eliot and the youthful home of Tennessee Williams.

Somewhere in the circle created by this sector lies the hamlet of Cossins, Missouri, originally known as Cossins Crossing. Cossins Crossing, somewhat like a pupa, metamorphosed over a century or so into the town of Cossins which in turn transformed itself from a sleepy corn and cattle station not to a city but to a kind of semi-sophisticated shire town with a courthouse, college, and two hospitals, one for the mentally ill called in earlier and less euphemistic times an asylum.

It is to this birthplace that my sister, Edith Endsley, returned in March of 1946 from her duties as a WAAC, an army nurse in the Pacific Theater of World War II. My name is Elizabeth Endsley. I'm Edith's younger sister. I wanted so terribly to be what came to be known later as a WAC, to be like my sister but, by the accident of birth that charts the courses of us all, it fell to me to study the war rather than participate directly. Indirectly, however, along with the others of our grades, we memorized aircraft silhouettes—enemy and ally—collected newspapers, bought war bond stamps, and scoured the sidewalks and gutters for empty cigarette packages: the silvery paper inside was rolled into balls and sold for a penny a pound as a kind of aluminum substitute. And, of course, there were the weekly, random air raid drills that sent us diving under our desks and, for girls at least, tucking our skirts under our knees. It went without saying, although there was actually more than a little saying among the girls, that for the boys the drills were more for fun than for safety and involved our skirts under the desks more than the protection of our heads.

For the first few months—no, more like six or seven months—Edith and I spent long hours on the wide porch of our house together. It was June of 1946. I was a rising senior in the local high school and on summer vacation. Since March when Edith came home, she had kept mostly to herself and mostly in her room. Mom and Dad and I worried about her but didn't know what to do, what to say. Edith had seen a lot, we knew, probably too much, but her VMAIL (Victory Mail) letters on onion skin paper from places like Guam, the Philippines, or Singapore told us little of the hell of war. She'd had to respect censorship and the longer she was away the tighter became both her letters and her personality.

Edith stayed up late at night, alone in her room. I could see the light under the door on my way to the bathroom or, as she still called it, the head. I didn't know whether she was reading or lying in bed thinking about the war or planning her next move, her new life as a civilian. And I never asked her. Popular articles in papers like the *St. Louis Post Dispatch* had advised us for some time to let returning GIs set their own agenda, as they put it.

As I had watched her high school years from the vantage point of the younger sister of eleven, just moving into brassieres and lipstick, I'd seen at least superficially a girl who liked boys and dances and music and tennis, a tall, slim girl with a modest figure and a devastating backhand.

On the wide, wooden porch of our two-story town house Edith and I sat and talked and listened to each other. Two girls—no, although but five years apart, one girl and one woman of indeterminate age. I was shorter than Edith and on the stocky side. My figure was fuller but, in spite of the pull of culture, I took no pleasure in it. True, my hips and breasts were more, as they say, voluptuous, but they gave me the feeling of being stuck, set with them. Edith, I felt, could grow with hers or if she didn't it didn't matter. I could grow also but the thought of it was depressive. I was full blown at sixteen and my life, I thought, would be one of eternal physical containment, some sort of goodies-free physical and psychological containment.

So, as the weather warmed we sat longer on our porch, the porch that welcomed us then as young girls where Mother brought us lemonade and cookies and we played Pick-Up-Sticks and Chinese Checkers and Edith helped me clothe my paper dolls with proper outfits.

Now, with Edith home from the Pacific and God-knows-where, we sat on our porch and talked of her war and my last year at Cossins High and where we each would go. Talk of the war was not always tedious. Edith had drunk beer with her buddies, guys and girls, and paced the deck of the navy hospital ship USS Mercy, staffed by army medical personnel, with an ensign named Danny when the smoke of battle cleared for the moon.

We got our own drinks now, iced tea in a tall glass with a straw for me and Jack Daniels in a china tea cup for Edith. Mother didn't seem to mind. We lived in German beer country and there were always cold bottles in the ice box on the back porch.

The conversation surrounding me was, by comparison, quaint and, according to my sister, refreshing. Around age seven I'd developed an interest in jazz, collecting records and wearing out the radio stations in an obtuse triangle of Kansas City, St. Louis, and Chicago. Red McKenzie, who oddly enough played the comb and tissue paper in his very early jazz band called the "Mound City Blue Blowers," attracted my attention first because of love and loyalty for my home state and because he had co-written a tune with Gene Krupa called "One Hour." This early exposure to future greats like Chicago's Krupa led me to become the first girl lead drummer in the Cossins High School Marching Band.

"What year are you talking about?" my sister said.

I brushed my hair back with the first two fingers of my right hand, my thinking gesture. "Red started in 1923 with Dick Slevin on kazoo and Jack Bland on banjo. They made some records between then and 1929 when Red picked up other coming stars like Jack Teagarden and Glenn Miller on trombones and Coleman Hawkins and Pee Wee Russell on tenor sax and clarinet."

Edith frowned her version of disbelief. "Wasn't all that old stuff kind of corny, Sis'?"

I nodded. "It was, at first, although the really old stuff by men like Kid Ory, King Oliver, and Buddy Bolden really set the stage for the great big bands we have today."

Edie sipped her Jack Daniel's and twirled her china cup. "I wish we could have shared more of that together, Sis'. But my interest in early jazz at that time was about as keen as that of our long ago paper dolls. I'd finished my nurse training at Westwood College and could hardly wait to get to the WAAC Training Center in Des Moines. The girls—I guess I should say "women" because many of them were in their late twenties and beyond although even those were girls before the roar and the smoke of battle made them women regardless of age—who had their bachelor of science in nursing degrees bypassed the boot camp or basic training phase and were commissioned second lieutenants. I missed the boat so to speak on that one because although I had my degree I was just nineteen, two years short of the minimum requirement. One of the girls in my class at Cossins told me that her sister got in under age with a doctored birth certificate and that they needed graduate nurses so badly that they probably wouldn't pay attention to my age, certificate or no certificate.

A nurse with the rank of major pulled me aside and into her office. She sat behind her desk and I started to sit on the chair in front of her desk when she told me to remain standing. I was carrying my barracks bag with most of the twenty or so items of clothing issue I had just received. The major told me to set the bag on the floor.

"You're not twenty-one," she said.

"I know," I said.

"I know, Ma'am," she said.

"I know, Ma'am," I said.

I had shifted to one foot. "Straighten up, soldier," she said.

"I'm a nurse," I said.

The major studied her desk. "You're a soldier first, Endsley," she said. "There's no nursing without discipline. Your papers look excellent, third in your class at, what is it? Westwood College? Not too far from here, eh? You're tall, lean, look like you're at least twenty-one. Look, also, like you can move. Mmmm. Tennis team in high school. Sit down, Endsley."

I started to sit. "Yes, Ma'am, Endsley," she said.

I sat. "Yes, Ma'am," I said.

The major tucked a piece of hair under her olive green cap. "Endsley, to be honest, I like you. Actually, I'm not supposed to say that. The army's first concern is regulations, discipline. But, somehow, you seem to have . . . to fit. This is highly irregular but you have your degree and you look like a soldier. I'll make you a deal and if you ever mention it I'll have you thrown into the stockade. I'll accept you but not as an officer. As sergeant major you'll serve in the capacity of an administrative assistant. This will cost you some pay and some prestige as a soldier but nothing as a nurse. Do you understand, Endsley?"

"Yes, Ma'am. Major," I said.

"Do you agree, Endsley? About the terms, about your role, about your place?"

I smiled softly. I couldn't tell the major but she looked a little like Mom.

"Why are you smiling, Endsley? Is something funny? Stand."

I stood. "No, Ma'am," I said, "not funny, just lovely. I'd agree to almost anything to be here, to be an army nurse. Thank you, Sir, uh Ma'am."

"Relax, Endsley, you'll do well. I'm counting on it and I'm counting on you. And by the way, Endsley, nothing in the army is lovely. You're dismissed." The major swiveled in her chair to a mirror on the window sill behind her and tucked another piece of hair. I picked up my duffel bag and then dropped it. I saluted the major's back. She saw me in her little mirror and smiled. Again I picked up my bag, turned, and left the office.

Edie and I were still on the porch but we'd finished our drinks, my iced tea and her whiskey. I was about to take her cup and my glass into the kitchen for refills when she took my hand. "Come," she said, "I want to show you something." We walked down the hall to her bedroom. The feeling was magical. Here we were, sisters, a more than grown woman and an almost grown one, hand in hand as we had done probably thousands of times on our way through girlhood, walking not skipping this time but together as only girls can be together, especially girls who are sisters— perhaps years apart in age but tied as twins emotionally.

We entered her room as we had done so many times over the years and, automatically, I sat at the foot of her bed. She went to her closet and returned with her army duffel bag. Next to me on the bed she undid the cord that tightened the top of the bag. She chuckled. After so long without that chuckle I felt all warm inside. I edged closer to her until we almost touched. "I'm going to make you feel very lucky," she said. "No, it's more than that, Liz, I'm going to make you feel truly blessed." I wondered what was coming. Had she brought home souvenirs from the Far East? A paper fan perhaps? A kimono? A Japanese dagger? It all seemed so romantic, exotic.

Again she chuckled. One by one she pulled out first a jacket, then a skirt, a coat, two waists (I asked her what a "waist" was). "In this bag," she said, "are more than twenty items of G.I. Issue clothing—my whole army wardrobe."

"Are they all khaki?" I said.

"Every single one," she said, "right down to the underwear."

This time I chuckled. "You're kidding," I said. "Khaki underwear? I don't believe it!"

Edie grabbed a pile of stuff out of the middle of the bag. "How do you like this?" she said. On the bed was a pile of pajamas, slips, stockings, brassieres, bathrobes, and sweatsuits, all light-khaki color. "What are they trying to do?" I asked, "keep all the boys away?"

"This is every girl's complete issue and we're responsible for taking care of every item and before we can get replacements we have to prove an item is worn out. How do you like them apples, so to speak?"

I picked up a piece o Edie's G.I. clothing. "I didn't know the army was so androgynous," I said,—"soooo, well, dull. What is this? It looks like grandma's bloomers without the bloom, like someone let the air out of the tire."

This time Edie laughed out loud. "This," she said, "is what the army calls panties, down to the knees. Can you imagine? What girl would want her boyfriend to see these hanging on the line, let alone on her? They don't use many big words like "androgynous" in the army, Sis, but this dullness you speak of is absolutely essential to military success. Just as everything in the navy is painted gray, khaki is the uniform of the day in the army from, as they say, from caps to crotch. Not very sexy is it?"

I sat there on the bed, so-called panties in hand, feeling somehow embarrassed. Edie was twenty-one and I was going on seventeen and suddenly I realized I had thoughts about my sister that I'd never had before, thoughts of her as a woman, even as a sexy woman. For the first time since she'd come home—actually since she'd left two years ago—I thought about where she'd been, even what she might have done. The thoughts were uncomfortable. She was, after all, a grown woman but she was also my sister. I remembered how I squirmed in sixth grade in biology class when I'd had to come face to face for the first time with the reality of how I got here, with the mental picture of my mom and dad doing it.

"Liz," she said, "are you okay?"

I snapped to, as I'd heard Edie lapse occasionally into G.I. jargon. "Uh, yeah, I'm fine, Sis, just thinking about the army, the army and you, the rigidity. Does it change people, Sis, I mean does it change people permanently?"

Her hand had been on mine, on the one holding the khaki panties. She took her hand away and placed it with the other in her lap. She studied her hands as if she were going to sketch them. "It can," she said. "It can definitely change people, men as well as women. The rigorousness of the military, especially in battle, can confer a kind of protection that's welcome until the fight is over. Afterwards we sometimes find ourselves asking ourselves where the break is, where the tenderness is. The word "soft" does not come up very often."

"We think of the military, especially the men, as hard, don't we?" I said.

"They have to be," Edie said. "First tough physically, which leads easily then to mental toughness and then—and most importantly—to emotional strength. We, the nurses, learned that that's where we came in. The men, some no more than boys who'd never been away from home, not even to scout camp, came hobbling or on stretchers aboard our hospital ship, the *Mercy*. Most needed immediate physical attention to wounds suffered in island invasions or from torpedo or air attacks to their ships or planes. We saw, and we liked to think, although some of the men pretended otherwise, that in a sense we, the nurses, were the feminine yin for their masculine yang, the rest against the beat of the heart. We saw not only a place but also a need for the soft. After all, Sis, boys too were nursed and changed and bathed in the tenderness of woman. These strong men, battered and broken and bloodied needed their own kind of nursing, bathing and changing. The looks in their eyes of pain and gratitude and even love from some—these were our pay, Sis. After all, who is more like a mother than a nurse?"

I had been listening intently, staring at the knots in the wooden planks of her bedroom floor, feeling almost like I should be taking notes or memorizing every word. My sister, my older sister, was opening herself to me as one might with a scalpel and when at last I looked at her I saw the tears, tears that were perhaps not just hers but those of the men who had let her see them cry. Then she saw me see her and, for the first time in our lives she leaned against me and rested her head on my shoulder and I became, for the first time, the older sister.

We stayed that way for what seemed like a long time, the shoulder of my blouse damp, her beautiful head softly heavy upon my body when she looked up into my eyes and said, "No tears, no life." I knew then that my sister was home from the war for good. I did not know that other battles lie ahead for her.

TWO

Mom and Dad both grew up in our old house in Cossins, Missouri. Mom's name is Marie and Dad's name is Roy. They raised us both after Dad's parents, our grandparents, so to speak, had Dad the old fashioned way and adopted Mom after her parents died in a car wreck on a lonely, rain-splashed, unbanked curve of road between Cossins and Columbia, home of the University of Missouri where Mom's dad taught English and the history of what Mom said her dad insisted on always referring to as the great state of Missouri. So in simpler terms our mom and dad, Edie's and mine, grew up as sister and brother or, if you insist, as adopted sister and brother. Unintentionally, Mom and Dad fell in love when Dad went off to France in World War I to fight what he called The Hun and we called the Germans or Krauts or Heinies. They began by writing letters. Often the letters, both his and hers, didn't reach each other which caused them to write more often and to feel the frustration of being so far apart. It wasn't too long before the frustration turned to longing and then, in the realization that, after all they were not related, to the love of one to another as man and woman. And, of course that explains the two girls, Edith and Elizabeth Endsley, Sis and me.

Westwood College rises grandly on a hill at the end of Main Street. It is fairly typical of small, private colleges across the country, this one with a Presbyterian affiliation but not requiring such connection for admission. As opposed to the Land Grant Colleges established by the Merrill Acts of the mid-1800s which were basically agricultural and mechanical schools, small, private colleges offered primarily liberal arts courses aimed at the bachelor of arts degree. I know all this because I had to write a high school term paper on it and because after next year, my senior year at Cossins High, I plan to attend Westwood. I'm not quite sure but I think I'll major in English and then go for a masters at the University of Missouri (Mizzou) in journalism. Sister Edie had always been the science and numbers girl and I what I heard someone call once the wordsmith. I can't remember when I didn't like to write. When I was about eight years old Mom asked Sis and me what we wanted for Christmas. Edie was about thirteen at that time. She asked for a chemistry set. I asked for a child's version of a roll-top desk, a place where I could keep my writing supplies, my paper and pens and erasers and notebooks. I love that desk and I still have it in my bedroom. And someday if I'm not too big for it I'll at least start my first novel on it.

◇◇◇ ◇◇◇ ◇◇◇

Where Main Street ends in front of Westwood College it is crossed by a north-south road called College Avenue. Actually, few people call it by its name. The stretch north of Main Street is called Fraternity Row and the one south of Main Street is Sorority Row. There are six rather dignified fraternity houses on that row, some trying for regional identity with stately, white columns recalling the antebellum South and with names that the Greek Societies readily associate with an area of the country. It's important to note that all six of these houses bear names of national recognition because each house is supported by its national organization and not by the college. The same is true of the five sorority houses on the south end of the street. The college supports an equally impressive dormitory at the top of the hill for Independents, those who choose not to join a Greek society or are not invited. The Greek Houses draw heavily from family members who were and are still members of that House. The Independent Hall makes a satisfactory if not adequate attempt at pluralistic diversity by drawing from a more liberal base that may feel less need either of brotherly or sisterly love or for social finishing. It must be said also that the north end of the hall for independents is reserved for females and the south end for male students. The two wings are balanced by a large atrium containing a cafeteria, lounge, and ballroom for dances and other social activities. As a final note, and technically speaking, an atrium is a central room or courtyard in a Roman home.

The nursing department of the college enrolls chiefly girls who live in town, although they are free to pledge if they want to and are invited. Most of the pre-med students join a Greek society for the professional association and for the so-called "polish" they offer. The majority of nurses join one for the friendship and social aspects provided by a sorority. However, unlike home or Independents Hall, Greek societies are more expensive, charging not only room and board but dues as well. When my sister Edie studied nursing at Westwood she lived at home and, although she could not afford to pledge a sorority even if she had been asked, she had friends in a couple of the houses and was invited to occasional socials and to bring a date to a dance. Some Greeks are less exclusive than others.

Edie then was, of course, what they called a "townie." Both the town kids and the students seemed comfortable with this and did not see it as pejorative. Actually, it was a bit strange as the "townies" seemed to regard their lot in life as somewhat superior to the students and vice versa. It seemed as though the town kids saw themselves as freed from the slavery of books and involved with the real things of life like jobs and cars and money and family. The students, on the other hand, appeared to view themselves as making a sort of sacrifice, forgoing the fulsomeness of "the outside" (somewhat as in the military) to achieve the more esoteric advantage of delayed accomplishment. I guess it worked out well for both groups, who had, as they say, "Paid their money and took their chances."

Edie and I knew siblings like the twin boys down the block who seemed to have nothing in common and shared no closeness, no interests. We could never understand it, actually felt sorry for them, but, thank God and we did, this was not Edie and Elizabeth. We loved sitting in our rooms or on the porch even in chilly or rainy weather and talking.

Education, of course, was important to us. Grandpa had taught at the University of Missouri. His bachelors and masters degrees hung in the hallway, side by side and, although neither Mom nor Dad had gone to college, they were great readers and the house was full of books. Edie and I looked up to them and loved them and saw them, I think, as having a kind of noble, Abe Lincoln education. Oh, don't get me wrong, they both graduated from Cossins High but their unattained aims were much higher than that.

One summer day we were back on the porch with our usual drinks. Edie wore an army exercise suit and army athletic shoes. I asked if she hadn't had enough of that and she said she was still in transition. I wore a broomstick skirt and the blouse she had cried on that day. Her legs were drawn up to her chest, her feet on the edge of the wicker arm chair. I'd crossed my legs and was sitting on my feet watching a hawk circle the pond across the road. The sky was a blue the color of the Sheaffer ink we used to fill our fountain pens from the little bottles with the side well inside. A male cardinal sat on a branch of the big sycamore tree in the front yard and tweeted to his mate, his head bouncing from side to side. He knew she wouldn't come if she had nest work to do. I guess he liked to hear himself sing and probably knew we loved it too.

I don't remember why but once again the subject of education came up. We had talked about this before and I knew somehow we'd talk about it again. Our conversations were always exploratory rather than argumentative. If we didn't always respect each other's choices we did respect each other's minds.

We explored other aspects of education. Our parents had instilled the love for it, the value of it, the idea that, of all the riches of the world, it was the one jewel that could not be taken from us. But one of our favorite topics was the difference between education and training and, for that matter, did it matter. Our initial interest in this aspect of the process of human development started long ago, actually just as Edie was beginning nurses training at Westwood in spite of the fact that I was only thirteen then.

We discussed questions such as "Is nursing a training, an education or both?" "Is nursing a profession or simply a skill?" "Can a skill be also an art?" I think even at that early time that our interest, our fascination with the subject came also from the fact that it seemed obvious I was headed in a different direction from Edie's and that our love for each other did not want our careers to separate us in any way.

As kids do we were losing our way, getting in over our heads, so to speak. Things were getting thorny. The morass was up to our knees.

I said, "Maybe we should ask Dad."

"Yes," Edie said, "he always seems to be able to get to the heart of the problem. Why don't you ask him, Liz'?"

I found him in the garage working on the lawn mower. "Hi, Dad. What's up?"

"New spark plug, I think, and I don't have one. Let's get in the truck and go to town."

The short trip gave me half a chance to ask Dad about my talk with Edie and how we couldn't seem to work our way through the question. I could tell he was preoccupied with the spark plug, but on the way home he said, without looking up or even asking me a question, "Let me think about it."

When we got back Mom said Edie had gone down to Cossins drug store for something. I went to my room and looked up "education" in the encyclopedia.

I was again on the porch with summer lemonade when Edie got back from the drug store. "Good trip?" I asked.

"Yeah," she said. "I needed some girl things, time of month. Let me get some J-D. Did you talk to Dad?"

"Yes, seems he needed a boy thing, spark plug. He asked me to go with him. We talked on the way to town and on the way back. He is so good, interested in everything, especially ideas, especially what you and I are interested in."

Edie came back with her cup, a small, delicate white china cup she'd picked up in the Philippines. She took a sip and sat on her chair. "Hope this helps," she said. "It usually does. What did Dad say about our dilemma?"

"He said he'd like to think about it. Let's ask him. I think I heard the garage door close."

Dad walked up the sidewalk from the side of the house tossing a dirty spark plug up and catching it, over and over. I couldn't tell if he was thinking about the work he'd just done or about education and training. He took the four steps in two and sat on the railing in front of Edie and me. He kept on tossing the plug. He looked from the spark plug to us. "Well," he said, "from the motor of the mower to two lilies of the valley. Sure, and there'd be no beauty in old Cossins 'twere it not for the sunshine of your mither and the blossoms of me girls. And what'll ye be up to now?"

Whatever Irish we had in us was not very near the surface but Dad liked to try his brogue now and then. He was tall and rangy and always, except for Sunday, always wore faded jeans and, even in summer, long-sleeved shirts. Edie took after Dad and I after Mom.

"Edie's not feeling too well, if you know what I mean," I said. Edie reached across the drink table and chucked me in the shoulder. Her angular face pinked slightly and she picked up her cup. Dad took a second or two to size things up.

"Come now, ladies," he said. "Sure, I'm your paw, but I bought both of you your first ones. No need to be coy, now, is there? Edie, have you got a sip for your old dad?"

Edie handed the delicate cup to Dad. He took a sip and made that wry smile that everyone makes in the movies, including tough cowboys, that says it's good but it isn't water. The cup looked out of place in Dad's rough hand. He took another sip and gave the cup back to Edie.

I waited a minute and then said, "Can you help us out, Dad? They speak of trained nurses and educated writers. Is one personal formation better than the other or just different? We've done some reading of our own but can't come up with a clear answer."

Dad leaned his back against a white porch post and rested his left foot on the railing. A tractor rumbled past on the road and the driver waved. It looked like Mr. Geist from the feed store. We waved back. I could hear Mom in the kitchen with plates and I wondered what was for dinner.

"I heard you talking about this one day last week. You know how important your mother and I hold education to be so I stopped at the library on my way home. As you probably already know there's a lot of material on every aspect of education. I didn't have time to plow through all of it but I did find one fellow who seemed to boil it down the way I would.

First, he says that, with regard to careers, almost always both training and education are required whether it's teaching or nursing or writing or office management. He says the best example of pure training might be learning to drive a car as training asks the question *how* rather than *why*. But even here, he says, you can see that the *why* question may come up as in why is it necessary to relate the speed of the car to the distance between it and the car in front. Here's an index card. You can read the article for yourselves. Rest assured, however, that the career requiring more education than training has nothing over its opposite. It doesn't matter what career choice you make, you are still loving sisters and our choices belong to us. But for the sake of study just remember that training more often asks the question *how* and education *why*. Any questions?"

I looked at Edie and we held hands across the little table. "Thanks, Dad," I said. "You always come through." He hugged us both.

"I smell dinner," he said. "Let's go."

I put my arm around my sister's waist as we walked down the hall. "I hope I'm as good a writer as you are a nurse," I said. As far as I was concerned the issue had been resolved.

THREE

MOM CALLS IT THE GARDEN spot of the world. It's where they honeymooned and where, as little girls, we spent part of many summers. U.S. Highway 54 meanders southwest by way of the lovely town of Mexico then on to an oasis called Kingdom City, through Fulton and the capital, Jefferson City, known to the locals only as Jeff City, then to Mom's Eden at Bagnell Dam and the Lake of the Ozarks. The cottages were clean, airy, and rustic with indoor plumbing and a parking spot to the side. Steps and a tiny porch led to the front door. The early cabins stood alone before attached rows were built and a pool was added. Fishing in the lake was good and Mom was as good at it as Dad. We ate most of our meals in the cabin or picnic style on blankets in front although there were nearby restaurants with excellent fish and country style cooking and BYOB, setups provided. As Dad would say this was Middle American vacation at its best. There were always lots of kids to play horseshoes with or dive off the floating platform anchored in the lake. I was about seven and Edie twelve when she met a boy from Chicago on the platform. She told me later they didn't have much in common to talk about but she told him she wanted to be a nurse. He said he wanted to join the navy. Years later they met again on the USS Mercy. Edie was a sergeant major and he, Danny, was an ensign. I didn't tell her that I saw them kiss in the water. She didn't tell me, either.

FOUR

DAD JOINED THE FRENCH ARMY in 1917 just before the Americans, as the A.E.F. or American Expeditionary Forces were known, entered World War I. He drove an ambulance at Chateau-Thierry during the Second Battle of the Marne in France which became known as the first American victory of the war. His sidekick in the ambulance was a fellow named Louis Corcoran from St. Louis. Although Dad thought he saw medicine in his own future, neither of them had anything but rudimentary first aid training before going "over there," as the song said. Sulfa and penicillin were years away. Soldiers died on the battlefield who might have made it on the *Mercy* under Edie's care. Even though there were a few hospital ships converted from ocean liners, the task of ferrying the wounded from the battlefields inland to ships lying off the coast without the aid of helicopters meant that sustaining a serious wound with only the help of more than guys like Dad and Louis spelled death.

Near the end of the war Americans in the French army transferred to the American Expeditionary Forces for discharge to the United States. After the famous victory march down the Champs Elysees and through the Arc de Triomphe in Paris the various allied forces dispersed. Dad and Louis, along with all the other Yanks, were offered the choice to board troop ships for home or to receive their mustering out pay there, in France, and later to find their own ways home. Dad and Louis elected to stay in Paris. They found a very small apartment not far from the Place de la Concorde and decided to take up cooking and what Dad always referred to as the most beautiful language on earth, French, until they ran out of money and could book passage on a tramp steamer for home and for whatever work the bosn's mate would allow them to do. Dad and Louis were soldiers, not sailors, so in spite of doing their best the deck crew had fun with them, sending them on nonsense trips to places like the paint locker for things that didn't exist like propeller guns and shaving brushes. By the time Louis got home to St. Louis and Dad to Cossins they were absolutely out of money and looking for work. Louis Corcoran had a sister who was a lawyer in St. Louis, single, and with enough money to suggest that if her brother would share her home, the one they both grew up in, she would treat him to his dream of owning a small sailboat until such time as he would need to find a suitable career. Dad had a sister, too, but she was not wealthy and needed, wanted, Dad to come home to her for more intimate and enduring reasons. They had, as I've alluded to before, developed much more than the familiar relationship of brother and sister. In short, Marie Endsley wanted Roy Endsley to come home from the Great War, The War To End All Wars, and marry her. And, of course, he did come home and he did marry her and I, Elizabeth, and Edie, my sister are here, I guess, because Dad wanted Mom more than he wanted a sailboat or anything else on earth. As I said, he was broke and needed a job so he went down to the east end of Main Street in Cossins and applied for a job as a nursing assistant at the State Mental Hospital. The idea had not occurred to him before the war but it was steady work and the pay, while meager, was a start and his medical experience, although somewhat more than meager, gave him a foot in the door denied to most of the locals. Mom never claimed any records, world or otherwise, but she was fond of saying that there were probably not many women who were married without changing their name. Pulling your weight was big back then so Mom got a job clerking at the Five-and-Dime. Then Edie and I came along and Dad put in for more hours at the hospital. Moms staying home with the kids was also big back then. Louis, or Mr. C as Edie and I called him, trucked his sailboat down to Lake of the Ozarks from St. Louis once in awhile and we all joined him at the cabins. According to Dad Louis had been a good soldier but we never heard a word about his career so everyone assumed that he'd taken a permanent liking to his yachting cap, navy blazer, and white ducks.

The early French explorers left their marks on the Midwest of America with names like Jolliet, LaSalle, and Marquette in Illinois and Ste. Genevieve and St. Louis in Missouri. Near Lake of the Ozarks are the little towns of Gravois Mills and Versailles pronounced generally by the locals in the English of Gravoys and Versails. As is true of almost all French words Chateau-Thierry and Belleau Wood trip off the tongue with an unintended romance. Even the terrible battles fought there by Dad and Louis did not erase either the song of the language or the beauty of the countryside. When Edie and I were still little girls Louis had trucked his sailboat down to the lake and taken us all sailing. Edie and I were thrilled. Mom kept looking about anxiously, reminding us too often we thought to hang on so we wouldn't fall off which was understandable as we had not yet learned to swim.

We sat around the cabin in the evenings listening to Mom and Dad and Louis talk about the war and, especially, France. Louis seemed impressed with Mom's grasp of both France and the war. Dad had always been a private man and had kept even the general content of their letters to himself. Mom took a postcard out of her skirt pocket and handed it to Louis. It was a picture of the lovely Chateau-Thierry countryside. She said that it reminded her of the rolling hills around the lake and the dam. Next day Louis went into town in his truck. He came back with a thin oval piece of tree trunk. Someone had burned into the wood the word Chateau-Thierry. With the chain on the back we hung it on the wall of our cabin. We took it with us when we went home but ever after we got the same cabin, hung our plaque on the wall and always referred to our vacation spot as Chateau-Thierry. Francophile. That was Dad. Through all the scrapbook clippings, snapshots, conversations, postcards, and snippets of letters that Mom felt comfortable allowing him to share I wondered what kept Dad from never coming home, from spending the rest of his life in France. I was entering my second year of French as a high school senior and knew that Dad's pronunciation was as near as an American could get to a native. I felt that he must have absorbed the country and the culture through his pores. But his love for Mom, though shown mostly in subtlety in our presence, commanded his return to Cossins and to the woman of his dreams and his life. And, of course, Edie and I are here because he listened to God more clearly than to his own desires and I pray that he will never smell the powder at Chateau-Thierry more strongly than that of the beautiful woman he married. Even before I got to my own elemental study of French in high school, I knew that when Dad told me he loved me with his lips in English, his heart said, "J'vous adore." More than wine or the Eiffel Tower or the Arc de Triomphe or the magical Seine this man, my father, a small town boy from Missouri who carried the French soldier next to the American through cannon fire to help would forever embody to me the romantic, indomitable spirit of France.

◇◇◇ ◇◇◇ ◇◇◇

This time, though, that summer after Edie came home from her war there were just the two of us at the cabin, at Chateau-Thierry. This time we went down on the Greyhound. Edie had the money but had not yet picked out a car. The cabin, Chateau-Thierry, was furnished but we had to go a little ways to town for groceries and stuff and the manager, Mr. Branam, was always willing to hop in his truck and take us in, said he usually needed stuff for either the cottages or him and his wife anyway. He felt almost fatherly toward Edie and me after so many years and I found out later that Dad had asked him to look after us, keep an eye on us, and he did.

This was a talking time for Edie and me. Oh, we had talked at the house on the porch and taken long walks in the country outside of town but we both knew, as perhaps only girls can know, that we needed more, that the big one was coming, had to come to fill us out, to complete the picture that was and had been for all these many years a work in progress.

Each cabin was provided with two Adirondack chairs and there was always a collection of them down by the lake. The Adirondack chair is perfect for at least two things: the seat slants down to the back for relaxation and the wide arm pieces are great for drinks and snacks. That day we sat in the front yard in the chairs. It was morning and the surface of the lake shimmered in the early sun. I had tea on one arm of my chair and a Danish on the other. Edie had coffee on the right and on the left a rather large, blue book.

The marker sticking out of the top of the book was a St. Jude prayer card and it was near the end of the book. I thought I remembered that St. Jude was the patron saint of lost causes but I wasn't sure so I made a mental note to look it up in my saints book or sneak a look at Edie's bookmark later. Over the time since she came back home I thought I'd detected snippets of sadness even brinking on depression and I wondered if she had hooked up with Jude as a sort of substitute psychologist or counselor. I knew that there were service-connected counselors available for returning GIs but was not sure of my independent sister's ability or willingness to reach out to them.

"Good book?" I said.

Edie laid her hand on top of the book and stared at the grass at her feet. I thought I saw a tear in her eye, the left one on my side. I rested my hand on hers. "You okay?" I said. Still she didn't look up.

"I wonder what kind of man I would have been," she said.

"What kind of man? I don't understand."

"I saw them all," she said. "Different ages, shapes, sizes. Blonds, redheads, Negroes, Puerto Ricans. Some old at eighteen, some young at thirty. Some needing mothers, others needing girlfriends, most needing God. All needing me when they got to the *Mercy*. When they got to me and triage we, those boys and I, lost our modesty together. In one way or another I was either their mother or their girlfriend or their wife. They weren't sure what I could do for them and neither was I. The look in their eyes said, "Just do it."

"What about the eyes?" I said.

"The eyes," Edie said. "Some of those eyes. Some of those eyes were harder to look at than the torn arms and legs, than the holes in the chests. It was like the eyes that went to war, into battle with these men had been removed by a surgeon and reworked into tiny caverns of blackness by what they had seen, by what their owners had done, had done to them. To look into those eyes past the blood and the rearranged flesh and bones was to see a pain so black, so deep that only a man who'd vaulted the gates of hell and returned could know what awaits us on the other side of darkness, the darkness that lasts forever."

"What kind of man?" I said again.

"Yes," Edie said. This time she took my hand. "I had just pressed a stack of gauze pads into the side of a sailor I thought was unconscious, his white jumper completely red against what was left of his still white pants. I held the pads there, unable to move either for him or for me. I started to cry when I felt his hand on mine. Then he smiled. 'I love you,' he said, and died. It was then, at that moment, that I wondered as a woman what kind of man I would have been. There are those, Sis, who say that actually women are the stronger sex. At that moment, when that young sailor probably thought he was talking to his girlfriend instead of me I knew that I didn't care about who was stronger and I knew also that I'd never know even if I had continued to hold his hand and go with him to wherever he went.

"Then I felt a hand on my shoulder. Through my tears I hadn't seen Father approach. With his hand still on my shoulder he removed my bloody hand from the sailor's side. Holding my hand we shared the boy's blood. 'Let's pray,' he said.

"I couldn't hear Father's prayers through the pounding of the blood in my ears, but I could hear the guns roaring in the distance and, strangely, the guns of Dad's Chateau-Thierry."

We sat for awhile in silence after Edie's purging until her face was dry and I could tell it was time to shift gears. Finally, she spoke. "Liz," she said, "I'm scared. I don't know where I'm going, what I'm going to do.

Life looks like a mountain in front of me and I don't have the strength to climb it."

Again I took her hand. "Edie, really the world right now is your oyster, so to speak. You survived the war, probably the worst mountain the world has yet had to climb. I know it sounds corny but the glass is half full. You'll fill it up and not with tears of pain but with laughter. Your mountains are all behind you now. Whatever the future holds will be but molehills by comparison and you will step over them as lightly as we did the cracks in the sidewalks when we were little girls. Mom and Dad and I will be at your side always and, more importantly, so will God." I laughed. "Listen to me, the little sister, propping you up when I've seen nothing yet of life." I took her hand. "C'mon, I'll race you to the beach."

Edie won. She usually did and I usually blamed it on her long legs until many years later I learned that length of leg or, for that matter, of stride made no difference. It was in what they called turnover or foot speed that won the race. But this time I didn't care, really didn't care because my sister was home and she was safe and at that moment here by the side of the Lake of the Ozarks with our feet in the gently lapping waves I knew that to ask for anything more would be a sin.

We took off our wraps and tossed them on one of the chairs and for the first time I noticed that Edie was wearing a two-piece, something that our folks hadn't approved of. Oh, well, I thought, things change and after the war everything looked different to just about everyone and I knew that after what Edie'd been through, Mom and Dad wouldn't, couldn't, say anything.

We raced through the water to the platform and this time I won. We climbed the little ladder and Edie kept on going up to the diving board. "I haven't done this for a long time," she said from up top and did a perfect jackknife into the blue water. When she came up she was holding her top in her hand. She laughed. "Gotta get used to this," she said and climbed up on the platform, top in hand. Suddenly I realized that I'd never seen my sister's bare breasts before. They were smaller than mine but perfectly formed and I was pleased that she seemed comfortable like this, with me.

But then I remembered she'd been in the army and guessed that privacy was probably hard to come by there.

We ran our fingers through our hair and shook the water out. We sat near the edge of the platform Indian style facing the lake. Edie slipped into her top. "Hook this for me will you, Sis'?" she said and turned her back to me. At first I wondered why she asked because her bathing suit top looked just like a bra to me and then, while I fixed the clasp, I noticed that it was not a hook but more like a clip. This simple gesture on her part might not have seemed like much to anyone else but to me, an almost eighteen year old from her still young but womanly sister, it was a confidence unexpected and while only mildly intimate sent a chill up my spine and put goose bumps on my arms that at first I attributed to the cool water of the lake. It occurred to me that this could be an unintended invitation to a sisterhood of two women for the first time. I felt good. I took my time with the clip and Edie didn't seem to mind. Was this what was meant by the word *bonding* I thought. And then, how simple are the things of love.

◇◇◇ ◇◇◇ ◇◇◇

Edie and I had been at Chateau-Thierry for two days. We'd had plenty of time to talk—Danny Landy, the Chicago boy she'd met years before hadn't showed up although I thought I saw Edie look around a few times, especially when cars full of boys pulled up at one of the other cabins. We were sitting on the Adirondacks in the front yard when Edie said, "Out on the platform the other day we were talking about the muddle of my life when you mentioned something about an anchor. What did you mean?"

I took a sip of my tea. Edie had turned from her bourbon, at least in the morning, to coffee. "I remember," I said, "we were talking about your future weren't we?"

"Yes. And you hadn't finished."

"Strange. This anchor thing came from Father Bob at a meeting of the young people's group at church."

"Did it have anything to do with Noah and the ark? I always wondered if he had one, you know, to keep the ark from being washed away completely."

I chuckled. "No, it was an anchor for us kids, for anyone actually. Father said that, of course, the first anchor for all of us must be Jesus, must be God. Then he said that for mental stability it helps to have a second anchor, often called a gift. He said that everyone has a gift or gifts of one sort or another.

One of the boys asked why we need anything or anyone other than Jesus since we can do nothing without Him and everything with Him.

Father said that since everything comes from God the anchor is from Him as well. Perhaps, he said, we could think of it as sort of a rudder for our lives when things get stormy, when we are tempted to think we are alone. "Can you see where we are going with this, Sis'?"

"I'm not sure."

"I think it has to do with your muddle, as you call it. I think Father meant that of course we're never alone but sometimes it may seem that we're mowing up a hill that's too steep. We ask for help, say a little prayer for strength, but doing the job is still our responsibility. That's where the anchor may help."

One of the girls asked Father what his anchor was, when the hill got too steep, when the people in his life weren't working out. He said that it was a book he'd been writing for several years. He said it was a novel. One of the boys asked if it was sexy and everyone laughed. I was moved, of course, because I felt almost that Father had tossed the ball to me, hit the ball into my court, as a girl whose dream was to write novels. It was at that moment that I felt I knew what Father was talking about and also that I'd discovered what my anchor in life would be.

Edie set her coffee cup down on the arm of the chair. "And?" she said. She was wearing a soft, thin, terry cloth shorts and sleeveless top outfit. I would have chosen beige for mine, but the pale blue went well with her eyes and hung enviously on her slim frame.

I dumped the leftover ice from my tea on the grass. "And," I said, "when it seems like the patients in your life are not responding, Edie, in spite of your gifts as a nurse, perhaps it would help to have an anchor for your life or, as Dad would say, a way to drop back and punt."

Edie thought for awhile. Then she got up and went into the cabin, into our Chateau-Thierry. She came back with a white, porcelain cup like you find by the well. I could smell the bourbon. "And what would that anchor be?" she said.

"I don't know, Sis'" I said. "But it might be better if it was not a person."

She took a sip of the drink. "No?" she said. "Why not?"

"Father said the anchor should be something that is steady, something that doesn't shift, doesn't waver."

"I'll have to think about that," she said, and took a package of cigarettes from the pocket of her zippered shirt.

◈◈◈ ◈◈◈ ◈◈◈

Bagnell Dam and Lake of the Ozarks was close to but not exactly halfway between Cossins and Springfield, home of Drury College and where, at this time it turned out, Mom's brother, Richard Moore, lost to adoption as she had been when their parents died in a car accident was teaching English. Chateau-Thierry, our cabin at the lake, was a convenient stop at any time between Cossins and Springfield. And so, after their frequent visit to Uncle Richard at Drury it was both easy and natural for the folks to stop at the cabin especially as they knew Edie and I were there. Sis' and I had done a lot of talking and swimming and even diving (now, at least for the time being, she wore a beautiful one-piece, white with a flamingo on the front, the two-piece relegated now to swimming only). She said she had bought the flamingo at Kaycee Ladies Fashions in Cossins and was mildly surprised that the store had such stylish stuff until I reminded her that there were a lot of young women at Westwood College and also that there were also mature women like Mom who were not exactly stuck in bloomers and long sleeves.

I can't tell you how good—no, "good" is not enough—how halcyon were those kingfisher days shared at Chateau-Thierry by the lake between sisters loving and discovering each other bit by bit. Words sometimes escaped us but that feeling of closeness never did. I wondered if guys ever found that serenity between themselves.

"Uncle Richard couldn't come?" Edie said.

"Not this time," Mom said. "They asked him to teach a couple of creative writing courses for advanced regulars and local, Drury students. He sends his love, as he put it, to his beautiful and accomplished nieces and looks forward to seeing us all if possible over the Labor Day weekend. He also mentioned some of Dad's brats and beer."

"Is Uncle Richard Catholic?" I asked.

Mom said, "No, he was reared in the Episcopal Church."

"Is Drury an Episcopal school?" I asked.

"I think it's Congregational or something like that," Mom said. "But as I understand it even in Catholic colleges it isn't necessary to be Catholic. They look for the best teachers and try to get as many doctorates as possible both for ability and staff prestige. Uncle Richard is very good."

I brought up two more Adirondacks so we could all sit in front of Chateau-Thierry in a circle and talk and relax and enjoy the breeze off the lake. There was more activity today on the lake. Lake of the Ozarks is over ninety miles long and in the shape of a crescent. I don't care much for fishing but Dad says the largemouth and spotted bass are both fun and work to catch. I like the bluebirds and the flowering dogwoods best.

Mom and Edie went into the cabin. Mom came out with glasses and a pitcher of lemonade. Edie brought her big, blue book, a metal cup of whiskey, and her cigarettes. She laid the book in her lap and the cigarettes on the arm of her chair.

Blue smoke from Dad's cigar rose into the air like a column of fine cotton candy. Trying and not completely failing he dropped into his Irish side. "And just what have my pretties been up to this past week?" he said.

I waited to see if Edie wanted to answer. She lighted a cigarette and stared at her feet. Too much silence is not the best thing at a party and this was a family party of sorts, as it seemed always to be when the four of us got together. A motorboat hummed out on the lake and a mockingbird tried to imitate the sound. A mosquito circled Dad's head attracted perhaps I thought by a dab of Brylcream, but the smoke from the cigar sent the critter searching for a better rental. Mom sipped her lemonade. She didn't mind a good drink now and then but for her it could never be a regular thing, something from the past she said once but would never elaborate on.

I spoke. "Well," I said, "there's been swimming and diving and—I chuckled—Edie lost her top." Mom smiled, Dad looked away. "No boys around, thank God. No boys at all actually. It's been good, just the two of us. We've been eating well." I patted my tummy. "Mr. Branam took us into town for pizza and supplies." Mom looked at me as if to say she knew there was more. "And, of course, there's been talk, a whole lot of talk. Right, Sis'?"

Edie didn't say anything so Mom said, "The blue book, Edie. I've noticed it's almost a constant companion."

Edie handed the book to Mom. She read from the cover, "*HISTORY of WORLD WAR II.*" And at the bottom, "*ARMED SERVICES MEMORIAL EDITION.*" Mom opened the book. I was sitting next to her. I could see the pages. The first three pages were titled SERVICE RECORD with a square for a snapshot and lines indicating NAME, BRANCH OF SERVICE, RECORD OF TRAINING AND DOMESTIC SERVICE and RECORD OF FOREIGN SERVICE AND COMBAT. At the bottom of each page was the line for RELEASED FROM SERVICE. Edie had not filled in the page. Mom turned the page. Opposite the title page was a painting in color of the raising of the flag on Mount Suribachi. At the bottom of the picture were the words, "World War II's Most Famous Picture." And beneath, "Iwo Jima, 1945." I looked at my sister. She was crying.

Dad pulled his chair close enough to Edie so that he could hold her hand. He took a sip of her whiskey. She dabbed her eyes with the sleeve of her shirt. "Turn to the Foreword on roman page five, Mom," she said. It's written by a man named Francis Miller. Please read just the underlined parts. I think it may be the ultimate summary of human misery."

Mom started to read:

> We have lived through the most stupendous struggle in the 7,000 years of recorded history. The destiny of 70 nations and 2,000,000,000 people has been at stake. The homelands of more than three quarters of the population of the earth have felt the iron heel of war. More than 1,000,000,000, one out of every twenty human beings on the globe, have been engaged in the fighting forces of belligerent nations . . .
>
> The official lists of numbers killed and wounded are a tragic commentary on civilization: More than 20,000,000,000 casualties; 30,000,000 more men, women, and children driven from their homes; 10,000,000 more massacred; hundreds of thousands of homes left in ruins . . .

I looked at Edie. She was shaking. Dad gripped her hand.

> The cost of this "War for Survival," with its destruction, devastation, and economic losses, is estimated at the sum of $1,000,000,000,000.
>
> This is the price we have paid for human freedom. The amount of money consumed in this war is sufficient to build a home for every family in the world, or to give an education to every child on earth. It is far greater than all the moneys ever expended for schools, churches, and hospitals since the beginning of the human race.

Mom slipped a piece of tissue at her place, went to the kitchen, and returned with a cup of what I couldn't see but knew was probably whiskey. Dad and I sat still, staring at each other and probably wondering both what had happened to our precious Edie and also what her future held. Mom continued reading:

> Another war on this gigantic scale, with further development of instruments for destruction by scientific genius, would place the human race in danger of self-annihilation. Therefore, a clear understanding of World War II is essential for our own self-preservation . . .
>
> The colossal magnitude of this war may be visualized when we state that the armies and navies engaged in World War II would form a marching line of men in combat reaching four times around the earth in continuous procession.
>
> May it never happen again.

Mom closed the book but did not immediately hand it to Edie. In our circle we sat in silence. "Of course I knew it was horrible," Mom said.

Dad released Edie's hand and ran his through his hair. I could see a little water forming in the cups of his eyelids. "Mr. Miller certainly takes the world's biggest ogre and paints him as I didn't know possible."

At first there was nothing from Edie. She looked pale and seemed almost as though she were somewhere else. Then she looked at Dad. "Will I be okay?" she said and sat in his lap, her head on his shoulder.

◇◇◇ ◇◇◇ ◇◇◇

We sat there in our Adirondack circle for a long time in silence. A sailboat came too close to the dock and we could hear the rush of the wind in its sails. A portable radio on the boat played Frank Sinatra singing, "All of Me." A cardinal and his wife lit on the railing of the porch. I sensed that we all wanted to move, to break the grip of the war words of Francis Miller. I guess we sat there because we knew that when the next move came it would need to come from Edie who looked like a tall baby on her father's chest. There we were a family of four floating on the words of war so powerful that they forced the mind into banality.

31

No one said a word but we all knew that only Edie could come close to the meaning of the words of Francis Miller including Dad who'd seen his own hell in The First War, the War to End All Wars, the precursor, the horrible appetizer for the meal that our Edie had tasted. It seemed natural that she went to Dad. Mom and I couldn't understand. Oh, we'd seen the pictures too, the ones Dad never wanted to show anyone, of the German soldiers in their distinctive, actually better looking, helmets peering through a thin clump of thicket too sparse to hide them, their eyes staring, bloody holes that in the pictures looked more like huge black eyes looking, even waiting for the medic to come to take their guns away and take them home to their mothers and girlfriends. I wanted to but never did ask Dad who took the pictures and why he kept them. I guessed that just before they died they might have been aiming at Dad to kill him. We only saw the photographs once—black and white eight by tens—before they went back into the folder on the top shelf of Dad's closet.

◈◈◈ ◈◈◈ ◈◈◈

Edie stirred. Dad picked her up and set her on the grass. Mom looked at me, the only time she ever looked at me with eyes I could not read. "The lake looks good," she said. "How about a swim?" Mom and Dad went into the cabin to change. Edie and I had our suits on under our shorts sets. Mom turned at the steps. "No diving," she said. "I see some boys on the platform."

I laughed. Edie turned pink. I wondered if that day when she seemed to be watching for boys getting out of their cars if she were looking for someone to talk to, someone who could understand. Maybe even her young ensign, Danny Landy.

Dad went to town for pizza and beer. There was no diving but the swimming was good and a couple of the boys were interesting. Fortunately, none of them had been to war—Edie didn't need any more of that, certainly not today. Mom wore her usual blous-on swimsuit—her top,

32

like Edie's was modest—but it was new, a striking blue that complemented her eyes. Edie and I wore one-piece suits and Dad a pair of trunks with small, white tennis racquets on them. The cool water cleared our heads, the sun brought us back from the chill of Edie's blue book. The afternoon was definitely a gift from God for the Endsley family exceeded only by the presence of my lovely sister about whom I was starting to worry much more as I watched her struggle to shed the skin of what she'd seen and, for all I knew, done. I sensed that the time was not too far off when Edie's personal story would come and would trump Mr. Miller's blue book story, for our family if not for the world. Edie's story, unless she wrote it someday, was for us, for her, while Mr. Miller's story, as he himself said, was for everyone old enough to read or to hear from their parents if the earth was to remain green and walkable.

As we sat again in front of the cabin, Chateau-Thierry, eating a piece of pizza and drinking a beer (I was allowed one beer only to feel part of the family), the subject of sunburn came up as we had all taken too much sun and failed to lather up before going out to the platform. Mom said, "Calamine lotion is all I have in my bag. Is that okay?"

Edie said, "I have a small bottle of baby oil and iodine if anyone wants to share." Dad said he'd go with his tried and true cocoa butter and I said I'll take whatever's left if there is any. Actually, I preferred witch hazel but forgot to bring it. It seems that suntan lotion is like morning eggs—everyone has his own preference.

❖❖❖ ❖❖❖ ❖❖❖

It was Sunday morning. Edie and I had stayed up late Saturday night talking. She smoked and did a little drinking. I didn't push it, didn't really even look for it but I wanted always to leave the door open for the story, her story, that I knew would come, had to come. I'm not particularly fond of repeating themes but again, even at the possible expense of redundancy, I must say that surely there cannot exist anything more beautiful than the human sisterhood. I suppose that the ultimate

33

humanhood must be what Mom and Dad have in that consummation of the human experience called marriage or, in our church, matrimony.

"Mom and I have to go back home after lunch," Dad said. "Let's go over to St. Pat's to Mass in Laurie and then you girls pick a lunch spot. By now you probably know the area better than we do. I'll bring you back here after lunch."

"Sounds good," Edie said. "I need to find my skirt."

The Mass is a mystery and it is a mystery without solution. Because it is a mystery no one understands it, not even the pope. Someone has called it a trip to Calvary, a going back through the ages to the original Mass, Christ's sacrifice at Golgotha. Like the birth of a child the Mass almost always expresses and confers a feeling of, not happiness, but joy. When I was young, in Sunday School, Sister reminded us of the difference between happiness and joy: happiness, she said, comes from happenings like new bicycles and birthday parties. Joy comes, she said, from Jesus. She said that the only way to identify, to communicate with our Lord's Passion directly is through the Mass and that to miss Sunday Mass without justification is a mortal sin. When one of the boys in the class asked what about prayer Sister said that our personal prayers were wonderful, powerful, but that they were like the preface to the meal, sort of like the appetizer. I thought that was a bit strange but at least I understood what she was talking about so I didn't say anything.

The priest that Sunday at St. Pat's was a visiting priest with a French accent. That seemed to please Dad. It made me think of our Chateau-Thierry, and I decided right then and there that I would study French in college—Mom had insisted on Latin for high school.

After Mass, as usual, our smiles were ready and our hearts light. Dad treated us to lunch at a local barbecue place (no beer on Sunday). I had grilled chicken breast with baked beans and French fries. Edie had barbecued pork and Mom and Dad had the beef. It was good. The iced tea was a bit too sweet but it was always fun when the four of us shared lunch at home or out.

Mom and Dad took us back to the cabin, packed up for home, checked to be sure we had return bus tickets and slipped us each an extra five. In spite of my tears, always tears at any parting, I smiled with Edie and waved as Mom and Dad crunched down the soft gravel driveway and headed for route 54 and home.

◇◇◇ ◇◇◇ ◇◇◇

I didn't expect it so soon but it wasn't a complete surprise either. We'd planned on going home Monday evening but it wasn't meant to happen. I'd thought about the story, Edie's story, that I didn't yet know but knew was there inside her, waiting, needing to come out. I don't remember when I first had the idea that there must be one or where it would happen. I thought maybe at home on the porch or at the kitchen table. But then I worried about Mom and Dad: if they were present would the complete story come out? Dad had been through the First War and Mom was a grown woman who had borne two children but would that prepare them for the details that could come out of Edie's story? Edie had been an army nurse and we'd learned some things from the parts of her letters that were not blacked out but somehow I got the idea that even if there was only one version of Edie's story to be told it might be best told just between us sisters.

Monday night instead of riding the bus home Edie and I sat once again and for the last time that summer on the porch at Chateau-Thierry. Mr. Branam, the cottages' manager, let us stay the extra night without charge and we had a little pizza and a couple of beers left and Edie raised me a level by handing me one of the last two bottles. Mr. Branam said that Monday nights are always lonely as most everyone, like Mom and Dad, has cleared-out for home. The lake was like that, too, calm. There was no breeze as though it, too, had decided to go home to wherever breezes live. There were no boats so the platform idled as if waiting alone for swimmers and divers to come and fulfill its purpose.

We sat in the Adirondacks. It was hot. Edie had saved all her government issue clothes and had lent me her olive drab p.j.'s. She said they weren't issued nightgowns so she wore her olive slip. On the left breast of her slip and over the pocket of my pajamas were stenciled the letter "E" for Endsley and the last four digits of Edie's army serial number. Edie looked pretty in spite of her olive drab. The slip was, of course, not sheer but it was light and the hills and valleys of her slim figure could attract any man. Pajamas were still more my thing—Mom was nowhere near encouraging male attraction—but it was okay with me as my figure was fuller and I had not yet come to grips with owning what God had given me. We had not spoken for awhile. I listened for my bluebirds but nothing. Apparently, they were doing their version of Adirondacks and beer.

Edie had gone to the bathroom and had come back with her cigarettes and porcelain cup of what I couldn't see but knew must be whiskey. She was backlighted as she came through the door and it looked like she might have forgotten her panties but it didn't really matter, I thought, did it? I was about to learn how much it didn't matter as she sat down, lighted a cigarette and began to speak.

"Taiko," she said.

I said, "What?"

"Taiko," she said. "That's how it all started. Mom and Dad don't know. I spent three months in Zentsuji Prison on Shikoku Island. The Japanese forced their Korean troops to bayonet more than one hundred fifty British and American troops to death."

"Where is Shikoku Island?" I said.

"It is one of the south islands of Japan, small, only a bit larger than our lake here." She was staring at the lake. She lighted a second cigarette and took a sip of whiskey.

"How did you get there?" I said. "Why?"

"We were lying off the island, at anchor. We were waiting for wounded to be brought aboard the *Mercy*. A Japanese officer came aboard from a small launch. He said that some of the wounded were too serious to be brought to the ship, that at least one doctor and several nurses were needed ashore. He also requested a priest which at first seemed odd and later proved tragic. One doctor, three of us nurses, and Father Jim went ashore in the Japanese launch, a mistake that would cost the nurses our uncorruptness, the doctor and Father Jim their lives, and our captain his ship and eventually his career."

I studied Edie, my sister. With each sentence, almost each word she slunk farther down in the Adirondack chair as if hiding from her past. I wanted to ask her if she wanted to stop, the color draining from her face, the tiny beads of perspiration forming on the fine, blonde hairs of her arms. The tan we had acquired at the lake seemed to fade from her face and from the wedge between her breasts. I was worried. But she showed no signs of fear of her story. She breathed more heavily and a bit faster as she talked and I knew that this was, this story, the purgation that had to come either to free her or trap her in the past. I put my hand on her left arm. She looked at me as if for permission to continue, her eyes wider than usual. I patted her arm. She laid her head against the back of the chair and closed her eyes. I said, "Potty," and went into the cabin.

There were two beers left in the refrigerator but I felt constrained by family dictum to act my part, parents present or not so I took a ginger ale and returned to the porch. Edie was pacing up and down the porch but when she heard the screen door slam she sat down again in her Ad' chair. The humidity had risen as evening grew causing pole lights around the little village of cabins to sprout halos. I offered Edie my cold drink for a sip. She declined by tipping my bottle with her whiskey cup.

"The Japanese launch headed for shore, the officer in the bow, the cox'n at the helm in the rear. We stepped out of the boat into shallow water and onto the beach. Several Quonset-type huts stood maybe fifty yards from the water. The officer led us to the nearest one painted strangely with a Japanese Rising Sun to the side of the door and a Red Cross at the top of the curved roof. Inside was dark and we struggled to adjust our eyes. Against both side walls were small bleachers. Between the bleachers were banks of what looked like votive candles. I thought of our Catholic church in Cossins. We would learn very shortly that what was about to happen here was a service of depravity, of vileness designable in our time only by barbarians under the red sun of the east or the swastika of Europe."

The combination of humidity and evening had cooled our porch. I asked Edie if she was comfortable, a sweater perhaps. Her nipples had tensed against the slip. Mine had, too, but the pajamas had pockets.

"I'm fine," she said. "The anger under this story keeps me warm. Hatred is not a Christian thing, a Catholic thing. I must go to Confession soon.

"The bleachers were filled with Japanese soldiers. It was dark with only the candlelight but I could see the grins and hear the nervous chatter of anticipation. Suddenly it came to me: this was to be a show, a carnival, a Japanese version of Bob Hope and the U.S.O. I wanted to run, to scream. One of the nurses did scream and the reaction was chilling. The soldiers pointed at her, laughing. The meaning was clear. They wanted her first.

"But they didn't get her first, at least not in the manner they envisioned. The officer who had brought us ashore spoke pidgin English. He stood next to the nurse who screamed. He ordered her to strip. At the same time he told the priest to strip, also. For some reason, perhaps to avoid dealing with the hideousness that was unfolding before us, I began to think of the wounded. Where were they? In another building? In mass graves? Had they, too, been, bayoneted? We had heard and had been warned of the Japanese fascination with the bayonet. Part of the training for troops going into the Pacific Theater was a brief course on Japanese history and culture. I thought about hara-kiri, literally the cutting of the belly. Again, the knife, the sword, the bayonet." This time Edie turned to me, perhaps sensing that the five-year age gap between us might be too much to prepare me, sustain me for the blood that was war. "Are you alright?" she said. Actually, I was afraid for her, for what reliving this horror could do to her.

"I'm okay," I said. "I know that Mom and Dad wouldn't approve but I wonder if I could have a sip of your whiskey."

Edie looked into her porcelain cup. She twirled it and apparently decided that it was almost empty. She got up to go to the kitchen. "I'll be right back," she said. I watched her through the open screen door against the kitchen light.

"I think your panties are on the bed," I said.

She returned with the cup. She handed it to me. "Go easy," she said. I took the cup, my nose against the rim. I grimaced. The smell was overcoming. I had asked and even though she was my sister I knew I had to sip. I sipped. I handed the cup back to her.

"Can you ever get used to that?" I said.

"They say you can get used to anything." She held out her hand. "Cigarette?" she said.

"I've tried that," I said. "No thanks. I think I'll stick to my Hersheys and ginger ale."

"Shall I go on?" she said, studying my face.

"Please."

"The nurse stripped, her clothes falling softly to the wooden floor. The soldiers clapped and stomped their feet. For the Japanese the catcall was not an expression of disapproval. I died for her.

"The priest refused to strip. The officer in charge ran a bayonet up the back of the priest's shirt and tore it off. Father Jim was short and slightly built. His skin was untanned. The soldiers booed, apparently making fun of his pale skin and unmuscular frame.

"Again the officer ordered the priest to strip. Suddenly, I was gripped by the unspeakable. The officer intended to force the priest and the nurse to couple right there on the floor of the Quonset hut."

I stood up and stretched. I sat on the porch railing facing my sister. I cried. She handed me a tissue. "Did they know?" I said. "Did they know about the priestly vows, about celibacy?"

"I don't know," Edie said. I was in shock. This was not the physical and moral brutality of tossing Chinese and Korean babies into the air and bayoneting them as they fell. But it was another side of what we'd heard, of Nazis making lampshades of human skin, of forced prisoner marches of days in scorching heat on a teacup of plain, often rancid rice. As I stood there not wanting even to think of what would happen next, the absurd occurred to me: What we'd heard about the Nazis and the

Japs, that is about the atrocities, appeared almost like Hitler and Tojo were operating like two football coaches using the same playbook but still trying to outdo each other. I prayed. I thought that if Father were forced to go through with this, if he were able to go through with it, it would not be a violation of his vows, could not be under pain of death."

"But what about Saint Maria Goretti?" I said.

"Strange," Edie said. "There, in the heat and horror of that Japanese Quonset hut all I could think of was that young girl, Maria Goretti, who died rather than submit."

I slid off the porch railing. I stretched again and felt something against my left breast. I fished it out of the pocket. It was a book of matches. I handed it to Edie. "Here," I said, "I think these are yours. I think I'm ready for bed, hope I'm ready for bed. Maybe we should sleep in Mom and Dad's bed. I fear an attack of nightmares. What happened to Father Jim, to the others, to you? On second thought I'm not sure I want to know."

"There's more, Liz'" she said, "lots more." She drank off what was left in her cup, stubbed out her cigarette, and held the screen door for me.

Edie was right, there was more. We decided, after yesterday's heavy Monday, to take a break, not to discuss brutality on the bus ride home that Tuesday. We did not decide on a place or a time and we agreed that we had to protect Mom and Dad from the more gruesome parts of Edie's experience in the Japanese prison, but we both knew that we'd gone too far now to turn back. Looking back later I was amazed at our gullibility in thinking that a girl and a young woman needed to protect their parents from the facts of life, even the facts of their older daughter's life, facts we had already assumed they didn't know.

The ride home was nice. The bus was packed so any discussion of personal matters was impractical anyway. We met two young soldiers on their way to some new assignment in St. Louis. They were in uniform. They asked where we were going and we told them. I did most of the talking. They said they wished that they had time to stop over in Cossins, that they would take us out to dinner. At first I thought it strange that I showed the most interest in them but then pictures of Edie's hell flooded my mind and I backed off. The last thing we needed, I thought, was a date, especially with soldiers: the army was too close for Edie and, for me, Dad would never approve. There was a brief stop in Jefferson City where Edie and I transferred to Cossins. The boys bought us a Coke. They said maybe they'd look us up some weekend on a pass. Edie said nothing. I said thanks for the drinks.

FIVE

I T WAS THE FIRST DAY of my last year of high school at Cossins High in Cossins, Missouri. Outside of graduation day is there a better feeling? I wore a white dickey under a pale blue cardigan buttoned up the back that I slid into like a pullover. Edie was dressing also but it was not considered hip to have someone button the sweater for you. Over the sweater I pulled a box-pleat plaid skirt as close to the blue of the sweater as I had. Wardrobes were a constant study for us as the family budget was tight and the folks wanted us to put our studies first. Jobs for high school kids were not out of the question but the general emphasis was on family, fun, and flirtation. I sat on the bed to finish my outfit with white bobby socks and blue and white saddle shoes. I checked the mirror. I was ready for new books and my last year. I don't know what the janitors used but the best part of the first day in any school was the beautiful smell of the newly-oiled wooden floors, and the older the school the better. That smell and the smile of the first teacher you met in the hall were all that needed to be said about the first day of school anywhere in America.

Before I left for school I went into the kitchen to say so-long to Mom who was working on that night's dinner and to fish my lunch money out of the little ceramic dish at the corner of the counter. I was kissing Mom goodbye on the cheek when Edie came in. She had an interview for a job at the hospital at the east end of Main Street where Dad worked.

She looked smart in a new suit she'd just bought at Kaycee Ladies Fashions on north Cossins Avenue. It was green. The top was a sort of Eisenhower jacket ending just above the waist, a top made for slim girls like Edie that would not favor me or any girl with a fuller bust. The skirt stopped just above the knees and was perfect for business. We'd been taught both at home and at school not to cross our legs in formal situations but, if she forgot, the skirt would not betray her. My beautiful sister looked lovely but two things bothered me: her eyes seemed dull as if she might just be going through the motions and the lipstick was all wrong—too orange and way too much.

Should I say something? Would Mom say something? Psychologically, Edie was riding one of those shaky little trains at the amusement park as she tried hard to get her balance back after Zentsuji Prison. Before I kissed her goodbye and good luck with her interview I said I love you and handed her a tissue for the lipstick. I hoped but didn't know if she ever used it.

Dr. Sullivan was the superintendent of the state hospital for the mentally ill. His secretary ushered Edie into an office Edie said later was better suited for Samuel Goldwyn at MGM in Hollywood. Edie described it as plush and overdone but commented that maybe sometimes you only get to be the boss once in your life.

We sat on the front porch at the end of the day, this time with Mom. Dad was still at work. A pitcher of lemonade sat on the little table as Mom asked about our day. I could tell that Edie had spiked her lemonade liberally by the color the whiskey had added. I waited. I wanted Edie to go first.

"When I walked in he stood up, offered his hand, and pointed to a chair in front of his desk. It was a beautiful desk, I thought, of mahogany probably. He wore a suit and tie. I'd say he's about fifty or so, stocky, smooth black hair."

He smiled. "You're Roy Endsley's daughter, I hear. Fine man. World War I, I believe. And you're recently home from the Pacific."

"Yes, Army Nurse, USS Mercy."

"Was it rough? I offered but they wouldn't take me. I thought it was my age but they said, in spite of the fact they needed doctors, I was doing my duty here. Said they might be sending some veterans here, you know, mental cases, that sort of thing."

"Was it rough? It was bloody. It was loud. It was violent. It was horrible. But we did our best. Fortunately, I wasn't wounded." I crossed my legs. Suddenly, I didn't know what to say. He studied my application on his desk. He seemed more interested in my legs than in my application. I repeated myself. "I wasn't wounded. At least not that I can tell."

"This is a big hospital, around two thousand patients, greatly understaffed with about twelve physicians and maybe the same number of nurses. Three of the doctors are psychiatrists, four nurses are psychologists. As you may know having grown up in Cossins this is the first of three such state hospitals. The range of mental illnesses is not wide and some, like our alcoholics may be borderline. There are patients from around the state who do not even qualify as mental, from homes that either can no longer take care of them or don't know how. Back in the old days, except for our half-dozen buildings, this hospital is what would have been called an old folks home."

"Dr. Sullivan was actually putting me at ease. I thought that his rather lengthy dissertation might be an indication that he could offer me a job."

The doctor continued. "We operate under state regulations and policies and one of them is that we are discouraged from hiring members of the same immediate family. Of course, your father works here."

"I uncrossed my legs. I looked down at the plush maroon carpet. I could feel my face, my eyes, sag if not fall. I'm sure Dr. Sullivan could, too. I'd blotted my lipstick and mentally thanked you, Sis'. But I couldn't help feeling, as I do now and then, that not only the doctor but almost everyone else is looking right through me."

"Right now, "Dr. Sullivan said, "your dad is working the wards, the men's wards where, in spite of his medical training in the war, his military training lends him an air of stability and authority the patients seem to like and respect."

Edie sipped her lemonade and fished another cigarette from her pack. "At this point," she said, "I started to look for, if not silver at least some kind of lining in what I saw as a cloud hovering near the ceiling of the office."

"Unlike the old days," Dr. Sullivan said, "we have now a modern three-story building referred to as "the acute." This is basically temporary quarters for men on the second floor and women on the third who present with acute conditions such as appendicitis, gallbladder, and cirrhosis. The female nurse on the men's ward is near retirement. You are certainly qualified. The physical distance between the wards and the acute might easily serve to justify your position as a replacement on the second floor of the acute. This may take some study and some consultation." He looked at his watch. "Let me get back with you," he checked my application, "Edith." I stood up. Again, he offered his hand. Mine was sweaty but I extended it anyway. "I like your medical and military experience, Edith." He left by a side door. His secretary showed me out.

It was my turn now but I didn't want to go. I'd been interested in everything Edie'd had to say but suddenly I was ashamed of myself. It looked like she might get the job and I didn't want her to. Everything had always been Edie's and as she told her story I realized what was almost the unthinkable: I was jealous of my own sister, my lovely sister with the beautiful backhand. I wasn't aware that I'd thought much about it before but all these returning GIs with their ruptured duck pins in their lapels or on their shirt collars seemed to keep the rest of us younger kids in a shade that most of us hoped would lift after the war. After the war, I think most of us thought, it should be our turn to shine, to step into our own, so to speak. I had grown up in my sister's shadow, I'd known but had seldom admitted to myself, and now home from the war it looked like I might always be more Edie's sister than Elizabeth Endsley.

Dad pulled into the driveway. His long legs put him on the porch in about six strides. "Lemonade?" Mom said.

He kissed mom on the mouth and then Edie and me on the head. "Rough day," he said. "Think I'll get something stronger. One of the other ward guys was stabbed in the chest going through the chow line by one of the trusties who was serving mashed potatoes. The trusty is in lockup, the ward man is in the acute building waiting transfer to a hospital in Jeff' City. The trusty is a guy everyone seemed to like and trust, a black guy, mister five-by-five. I don't know his name but they call him Snowball."

Mom said, "Where did he get the knife, Roy? Doesn't look like he'd need that for mashed potatoes."

Dad sat on the porch rail, a water glass half full of whiskey in his hand. I envied him and Edie their long legs and lean frames and wondered if Mom did, too. "Don't know," he said, and once again a wave of Gary Cooper washed over me. "Somebody said he had it hidden under his shirt. Where he got it's still a mystery. We have to be on our guard all the time. The place can be dangerous, even the women. Liz', how did your interview go with Doc' Sullivan?"

Edie sipped her lemonade without the straw as usual and stared at the floor as always. I wanted so to help her come out of her cocoon. I'd heard the term "arrested development" recently in discussing GIs who'd left their developmental lives back in the war someplace. I wanted also to come into my own as an adult but, in spite of my newly discovered jealousy, not at the expense of my sister. Although there were no ruptured ducks after the first World War, I'd heard Dad say that the sheen on those somewhat proud pins would fade soon enough.

"I was nervous," Edie said. "But then, since I got home I seem to spend a lot of time being either nervous or numb. Doctor Sullivan seemed like a nice enough guy. I got the impression that if I hadn't been your daughter he might have spent more time studying my legs."

Dad smiled, somewhat sheepishly I thought. "With apologies to my gender," he said, "he's a man."

I couldn't picture my dad like that, as if he were like all men but under the circumstances I thought it best to, as they say, let sleeping dogs lie.

❖❖❖ ❖❖❖ ❖❖❖

Edie got the job at the hospital on the second floor for the men. She had two regular, daily, male assistants for each of the three shifts for which she was responsible, a nurse in charge of each shift. She was surprised when Doctor Sullivan made her supervisor of nurses and assistants for the entire acute building. She told Dad that she hoped it was not because she was his daughter. Dad said forget about it, just do your best. She told me she'd have preferred the third floor women's unit but that nurse was not retiring.

"Why," I asked her, "would you prefer the women's floor when most of your work in the army was with men?"

"That's a good one," she said. "I'm not sure. Maybe I'm a bit afraid that the men on my floor might trigger battle flashbacks."

"Let's hope not," I said. "Anyway, you got the job and I know you'll make us all proud, including Doctor Sullivan. And I think it's more than cool that Dad, a veteran of the first war and you of the second, father and daughter, end up working in the same hospital. More than cool, I sense the hand of God."

As supervisor, Edie was respected not for her age nor really even for her skills as a nurse primarily but for her war experiences: she had been tested in battle and had survived. She'd acquired a patina of maturity obtainable in almost no other way. Also, in her position she was required to rotate through all three of the shifts.

It was a Friday and Edie had the ten-at-night to the six-in-the-morning shift. There was no cafeteria for the acute building so Edie's job was a bag-lunch affair. Mom had packed her a tuna salad sandwich and some carrot slices and celery. She felt that that might not be enough to get Edie through the shift so she asked me to take her a plastic foam container of clam chowder. After all it *was* Friday. I told Mom not to expect me back right away as Edie and I could get into one of our long girl-talk sessions. And we did and that was when, as they say, the rubber hit the road.

"Thanks for the soup, Sis'," Edie said. The floor was quiet. It was about ten-thirty on a hot, humid September night.

I said, "You're welcome. Mom thought the sandwich and vegetables might not be enough. There's nothing like Mom's New England chowder. I had some earlier." I noticed Edie's cigarettes on the desk. "Are you allowed to smoke on duty?"

"Yes, with caution. Patients are not allowed to smoke. And, if you want something stronger than soup I have a locker in the coat room. Of course, the door is locked. I'd say that the theme here is quasi-military: keep a tight ship but remember that the boss is a superintendent and not a general. Anyway, so far I really like the job."

"Two things, Sis'," I said. "Back at Chateau-Thierry you said 'taiko' and 'combat knife'."

Edie lighted a cigarette, blew out that first blue cloud with the smell that even some nonsmokers can enjoy that comes more from the match than from the cigarette. Then she did that movie thing, dabbing a stray piece of tobacco from her tongue with a ring finger. "Strange, I'd almost forgotten. I'd said those without knowing it at the time as an opening for the conversation I knew we must have one day, the talk I guess we're about to start now. You'd asked about the doctor and about Father Jim and about the nurse who had to strip. Let me begin, then, with Father Jim."

I got up, pulled a paper cup from the holder, drew water from the large, glass bottle and sat back down. "Want something to go with that?" Edie said. I shook my head. I wondered if habits like Edie's ran in families, half hoping they didn't and yet curious. Edie stubbed out a cigarette that was still too long and began.

"We stood there in the heat of the Japanese hut. Father Jim's shirt had all but been cut off. He'd been ordered to strip but refused. Standing next to him was a naked nurse. As I look back on it these two, Father and the nurse, stirred some sort of sexual frenzy in the soldiers sitting on those bleachers. On the one hand it was clear that, in some fashion or another that nurse and probably the other nurse and I would be raped. On the other hand Father Jim, a Catholic priest, presented a confused antithesis to the soldiers. They were worked up and excited by both the situation and by the prospects that seemed to lie ahead. But Father's presence in black suit and Roman collar threw some cold water on the debauchery of the moment. It was a good bet that there were no Catholic Japs in the room but there was the sense that Father represented a good of some kind that, to the soldiers could be felt but not explained. At the peak of this emotional frustration a soldier charged out of the stands. He ran straight at Father. As he ran he pulled a short, wide-blade combat knife from a short scabbard or sheath. As a football player might run to block an opponent, the Jap hit Father jamming the knife into the priest's groin. Father Jim hit the floor, the soldier on top of him. Blood spurted in a gusher from the wound. The Jap rolled away on the floor, the front of his uniform soaked with blood. In anger he rolled back towards Father, arm raised with the knife to strike the priest again. Father lay in a growing pool of blood. The shock of all this threw the hut into complete silence. As the saying goes you could have heard a pin drop. The nurse had put her uniform on. She held her underwear in her hand. The officer reached the soldier with the knife in time to kick it from his hand. He slipped on the pool of blood and landed on his back. He reached over to put his hand on Father's neck. The priest was dead."

We sat in silence at Edie's desk for a long time, I don't know how long. Edie saw the tears in my eyes and patted my hand. She excused herself to the restroom. "Potty," she said. I got more water from the big bottle. Edie returned.

I said, "I don't know what to say. Have the folks heard this?"

"No. Just you."

"How can you . . . ?" I said. "How do you get over something like this? It must be burned into your mind . . . forever. Sis', I'm so sorry. I feel so helpless. Is there anything I can do?"

Edie put her hand inside the top of her nurse's uniform to adjust her bra strap. "There's more," she said, "lots more."

◈◈◈ ◈◈◈ ◈◈◈

In the time between our talk at Edie's desk at the hospital and Thanksgiving I had time to ask her questions about Father and the doctor and the nurses and about the soldier patients they'd been taken ashore to treat on the Japanese island. Father Jim, of course, had died and Edie said she never found out what the Japs did with his body. The doctor, when he found out that all the patients in the building behind the Quonset hut were not Americans or Brits or Aussies but Japanese he refused to treat them in spite of his Hippocratic Oath so they took him out behind the building and shot him. Much of all this, Edie said, was learned later back on the *Mercy* in bits and pieces of conversation after a commando-style raid actually under the direction of, Edie said, the great General Douglas MacArthur.

Edie had said that there was more, lots more, but it wasn't until Thanksgiving that we were able to pick up where we'd left off at her desk in the hospital. She'd bought a car with part of her mustering out pay, a green, used Oldsmobile sedan. I thought to myself that her age might dictate something snazzier, a roadster perhaps but then I remembered that we would never again be able to think of Edie's age as a number at a birthday party. The war and the wounds and the Japanese had stamped my lovely sister with a maturity she never expected nor asked for.

Uncle Richard had planned to come up to Cossins for Thanksgiving but he called to say his car was in the shop so Edie and I offered to drive to Springfield to pick him up. In return he offered to give us a tour of Drury College where I'd told him I planned to enroll the following year to major in English with an emphasis on creative writing, knowing of course that he taught both and hoping to get in early enough to beat the class size of twenty-five. When he asked about Westwood I said simply that I'd changed my mind. I left out the part about a woman's privilege. Dad said he'd drive Uncle Rich back to Drury as they had personal business to discuss, something about the family estate, he and Mom being brother and sister and all. It was on that drive that Edie continued her story and I got to know my sister better than I ever knew I could or wanted to.

Edie was driving. This time we took a different route. We were on US 63 headed south to pick up US 60 in Cabool and on into Springfield.

There aren't that many ways to get there but this was a change from the old US 54 to State 65.

I was waiting and then she said again, "Taiko."

"Taiko?" I said.

"Japanese drums," she said. "From as far back as the seventh century. Different sizes and purposes usually ceremonial or entertainment. They lied to us but what chance did we have but to believe them. There was the Quonset hut and behind that the building where the Japanese wounded lay and beyond that what they told us was a tea house where we could bathe and eat and relax to music and the melodic beat of the taiko drums. By then it was just the three of us nurses. Without saying it, it was clear that before we left the island, if we left at all, we were going to be raped. The officer said that there were three doors to the tea house but that we must use the one next to the naked window with the red drums in it. Why red drums, I thought. Why a naked window? What is a naked window anyway? Surely, murderers were not going to become hosts, I thought. I was right."

We stopped at a country store for gas and a Coke. While we found the restroom a young girl in jeans and a cowboy shirt went to the pump to fill us up. While we paid for our drinks and gas and made small talk with the elderly man behind the counter the girl parked Edie's car at the side of the store. There was a November chill in the air but we found a picnic bench in a patch of sunlight beside a grand old oak. Edie shivered a bit so I went to the car for our sweaters. The cold Cokes didn't help but they gave Edie a chance to continue her story before we hit the road again.

"I'm not sure of all this, Sis," she said, "because so much of it came later, either back on the ship or from research. It's possible that the red drums may imply a sexual or sensual intent. And there are basically two kinds of windows in Japanese houses or buildings. A kitchen window tilts out from the bottom but windows in other rooms slide laterally. A naked window is one that is open so that the view from outside is unimpeded.

"We did as told. We entered the teahouse by the proper door. A geisha played softly on the red drums. From somewhere in the back of the house came the tinkling sound of a high-pitched guitar or lute-like instrument. The air was soft but filled with the aroma of several different incenses. In spite of these first impressions the large central room was quiet. The incenses seemed both to cross each other and yet meld. It was the most tranquil and romantic place I'd ever been.

"There were three small pools. Kneeling by each was what appeared to be a geisha. We learned later that all of the geisha industry had been shut down by the war, forcing those girls and women into war plants. The three in this room escaped the factories by agreeing to become geisha of sexual favors here on the prison island. We learned that true geisha do not offer sexual favors but rather dancing and conversation and the veiled insinuation to the man that there might be something more later."

The sun had faded at the picnic table. Edie looked at me as if to see how I was handling what even I knew was coming. After all Edie had made it pretty clear that the end of this part of the story would be painful if not violent.

Edie continued. "Each geisha motioned one of us three nurses to her pool. We hesitated. In my mind and, I was sure, in the minds of my friends, the situation was both frightening and strange. Why women? I thought. Where were the men, probably the officers we'd created in our minds. The young Japanese women wore the traditional geisha costumes I'd seen in *National Geographic*. Their smiles seemed artificially pasted to their faces. The makeup was beautifully precise but way overdone. The beautiful black hair sculpted above their heads so deftly that, as a woman, I had to try to imagine doing it myself.

"Each of us stopped at the side of a pool. Each geisha rose from a kneeling position, her smile almost dispelling fear. I couldn't see my friends because each of us was facing a pool and away from each other. My geisha stood behind me. She slit my uniform down the back with a knife of some sort. It fell to the floor next to the pool. Next, softly, artfully, she undid my bra and slid my panties to the floor. I stood naked before my geisha who could see at that moment only my back. I guessed that the ritual was being repeated in unison behind me as a musical trio might perform. But I could only guess. The silence, in spite of the music, was ear-splitting, so I could hear nothing from the other two pools.

"Again, in my mind, where were the men? Were we for some irrational reason to be spared the men, the rape? Suddenly, the answer to that question seemed even more vague. Next to my pool and, I assumed the other two, was a narrow table covered with a bright red towel. My geisha motioned me to the table and to lie face down. The table was soft. At once I felt her hands on my back working warm oil of some sort into my tired muscles. In just a few minutes, or so it seemed, I was close to sleep and fear of the men, of anything really, had disappeared. Then she whispered something in Japanese that of course I couldn't understand in spite of having picked up a word or two in the course of following directions.

"She touched my shoulder on the underside and I knew she wanted me to turn over.

"Liz," Edie said, "I know you're a young woman but I don't want to take you too far. Do you want me to go on?"

I didn't know what to say. This was my sister, my flesh and blood. This story, and not only this part about the Japanese prison, and all of the background I'd learned from Edie about life on the *Mercy*, the wounded, the dressings, the blood, the tears descended on me like the proverbial ton of bricks. This was not just a story one might read in a magazine by a veteran army nurse. Sitting next to me in the car, so close I could touch her, lean over and kiss her on the cheek was my sister, a sister who'd left, gone away to war a thousand years ago and was now asking me if she should go on in consideration of my youth and relative innocence. What should I say, could I say? That I wasn't up to being the only person available to her unburdening herself, the only person at that moment able to assist her in what was sure to be but a part of perhaps a life of catharsis? Suddenly I knew that aside from God, I was, even more than our parents, the most important person in her world. I was overwhelmed with love for her, with duty to her. The engine of the car thrummed down the two-lane road and blew red and orange leaves into the air and across the shoulder. A sharp-shinned hawk swooped across the road in pursuit of some condemned creature, her chestnut breast blending with the leaves of fall. I swallowed hard. I dabbed at the corner of my eye with a tissue. My voice was uneven. "Edie," I said, "please go on." She studied me as if to be sure and continued.

"She started, my geisha, at my feet. My eyes were closed. I could hear only the sublime, plaited strands of unmistakable Oriental airs backed by soft, almost inaudible pats and strokes on the red drums. I'd never had a massage before but it was clear that my geisha was a schooled professional. I'd imagined that massage was something rough, something that boxers and other athletes went immediately to after the fight or the tennis tournament. This was nothing like that. Her hands were little more than butterflies dancing over my body.

"Standing behind me she moved then from my feet to my head. I could smell her makeup and perfume. Her delicate fingers on my forehead, eyelids, and cheeks put me so close to sleep that I forgot where I was, even what I was doing here.

"I came to as she began softly to caress my breasts. It was strange, Sis'. I had dated in school and in the army but, and forgive me if I'm getting too close, no one had ever touched my breasts before, no one of course except me. At first it was simply pleasant. Then she placed the palms of her hands on my nipples and massaged them in a circular motion. I shuddered and started to sit up. What did she want? Where else was she going?

"She didn't press me down, back on the table. She supported my shoulders with her arm and, from somewhere I couldn't see, brought to my lips a small, warm, china cup. All this time she had not spoken nor sung. I sipped and she lowered me to the table. I was naked but not cold. The last thing I heard was her humming, like a lullaby.

"I awoke, I don't know how much later, to a touch on my shoulder. It was one of the nurses. I was wearing a light, silk kimono. The two stood at each side of my table. My breasts were not sore but there was moisture between my legs."

Edie's right hand was in her lap, palm down. She was steering with her left hand. I touched her right hand. It was shaking. "Were you . . . had you been raped?" I said.

She paused. "I don't know, still don't know. We stood on the beach in our kimonos until the ship's launch picked us up. There was not a Jap soldier in sight. Our doctor was dead so I had to wait until we put in to port for an exam."

"And?" I said.

"There was no evidence of rape."

We passed the welcome sign on the city limits of Springfield, Missouri. "Home of Drury College" one of the signs said. Others listed various churches and civic organizations. I pointed to one that said "Fish Your Heart Out." We laughed. I squeezed Edie's hand. "Feel like fishing?" I said.

"After that story," she said, "I feel more like drinking."

"Maybe Uncle Rich has got a nip or two," I said, surprised at myself. Edie looked at me and grinned.

"One drunk in the family is enough," she said. "Better stick to your lemonade and chocolates." We slowed and eased into town. College towns like this one and our town of Cossins have an aura all their own I thought and, also, were Edie's words those of advice or warning? I'd have to think more about that, a lot more.

◇◇◇ ◇◇◇ ◇◇◇

It turned out that Uncle Rich did have a nip—or two, or even three. Actually he had a bar in the living room of his bungalow. And before we left for home I felt that he might have an eye for my sister.

I hadn't seen him for quite a long time. The last time he came to visit, maybe three or four years ago, I was away at camp as a counselor. He looked more like Dad than Mom, his sister, tall and rangy. More than a teacher he was a writer and so for me he might as well have been a priest. I asked him if there was anything I could do—or he could do—to assure a place in one of his classes next year. He put his arm around my shoulder. "Don't worry about it, Liz'," he said. "Good as done."

We walked to the car. "You ladies look tired," he said. "Want me to drive?" Edie handed him the keys. He opened the passenger side door and I moved toward it but he stepped in front of me and waited for Edie to sit. I opened the rear door for myself. Guess it pays to have been around a bit I thought as Uncle Rich backed Edie's Olds out of the driveway.

SIX

THE YEAR PASSED. I GRADUATED from Cossins High School in June of the following year with high hopes but without distinction. Mom was sewing and gardening and helping out at church. Dad and Edie were hard at work at the hospital. The summer was old fashioned: no trips, hot, languid, lemony. I missed Chateau-Thierry and the lake but I was up to my eyeballs in college paper work and writing another short story; like a long distance runner who has his eye on the marathon but not yet ready mentally, I hoped that my classes at Drury, especially those with Uncle Richard, would somehow pave the way for my first novel.

Edie and Uncle Rich started dating the Christmas after we picked him up for Thanksgiving. At first it was just dinners and walks in the park when he could get away. Even at that Mom was leery. I remembered, in a discussion some time ago about her brother, Mom's saying that Richard may actually be her step brother. After all, she said, your dad and I were raised as brother and sister and over the years these shaded situations, as she called them *can* cause confusion and even dissension among family members. Dad didn't seem as concerned as Mom but he did point out that Christianity in general has always forbade marriages between first cousins and between aunts/uncles and nephews/nieces. I didn't know what to say. I was too young really to say anything intelligent so I just sat there.

But when Edie and Richard went to St. Louis for a ballgame one time and didn't come home until Sunday Dad got interested, very interested.

We were sitting on the front porch that Sunday afternoon when Uncle Rich and Edie came driving up in Edie's car. My first thought was where was all this going to go? My second was why Edie's car? Surely Uncle Rich's car can't still be in the shop. I was probably a bit on the old fashioned side with our small town and Catholic heritage but I wanted to see my sister in the man's car with the man driving. I knew things changed but in mid-America change was not what you'd call a high priority.

Uncle Rich leaned against the porch railing. Edie kissed us all on the cheeks and joined Rich at the railing. Mom said, "You missed Mass. How was the game?"

"Our team won," Edie said. "And we went to Mass at St. Monica."

Dad lighted his pipe and uncrossed his legs. "I hope you stayed at the Chase," he said. "Best hotel in town, they say."

Dad was in the middle, Mom on one side, I on the other. Edie blushed. She smoothed her skirt and buttoned another button on her cardigan. She looked at Rich and patted his hand. "Daddy," Edie said, "forgive me for not calling. We were having so much fun. Time got away. Except for the lake it seemed like forever since I'd really relaxed and let my hair down."

I winced. It didn't seem like just the right time to mention letting hair down.

"We met a couple at the game," Edie said. "Friends of Rich. We'd had a hot dog and a beer at the game and afterward Rich suggested we get a cocktail and something light to eat. At the bar, which, by the way, Dad, was at the Chase, Denise invited us to stay with them for the night and we could all go to St. Monica in the morning for Mass. Of course, at Denise and Roger's house Rich and I had separate rooms."

The air began to clear a little. Mom went into the house for lemonade and some glasses. Uncle Rich hadn't said anything. Then, "Roy," he said to Dad, "forgive me. I should have known better, should have asked Edie to call."

Mom returned with the pitcher and glasses, poured, and handed them around. Things got very quiet. Dad studied the floor. The rest of us looked around for a diversion to avoid the thud of the drop of the other shoe, as they say.

Dad motioned for Edie to come to him, to sit on his lap. "I'm sorry," he said. He chucked Edie under her chin. "You're not a girl anymore, are you? And forget the remark about the Chase. I trust you. I've always trusted you, Hon. I guess Dads are Dads and their girls are forever their girls. I haven't forgotten that you were a soldier in the war, that you got the blood of how many men on your hands trying to save them and that, while that blood may have washed off your hands it may take time, will take time, to wash it off your mind and out of your heart." He hugged Edie and kissed her cheek. "I love you," he said. He took the neck of Edie's sweater and wiped his eyes. "And I want to dance at your wedding."

Uncle Rich left in the morning. He'd spent the night on the couch and was waiting for a fellow professor to pick him up on the way back to Drury. I had to go back too but I still had a couple of days and Dad said he could get off work to take me if it was necessary. Rich offered to let me ride with him and his friend and I thanked him but under the recent circumstances it seemed better to put some space between Uncle Rich and Dad's girls.

Uncle Rich saw to it that I started with one of his basic English classes and, best of all, a creative writing class. I was excited. It was completely premature but this was the start—not really the start as it began when I was a little girl—but the official start of what I'd hoped for, prayed for all my life: the writer, no, more, the novelist. I liked alliteration and now I could say that Mom and Dad would have both a nurse and a novelist in the family. Hallelujah! Let the good times roll!!

No wonder Uncle Rich's classes were so popular. There were fourteen students in my class, eight girls and six guys. They came from as far away as San Francisco and as near as Cossins. The dress was casual. Guys don't care that much but the girls, imago-like, moved from the dresses and skirts of high school into slacks and sweatshirts with the Drury logo on the front. It was time to become butterflies. Dr. Richard Moore introduced himself and told the class that he'd be comfortable to be called Dr. Rich or even just Rich. This, he said, was not M.I.T. and this was not rocket science. The kids laughed. It was clear that, although undergraduate, Uncle Rich wanted this to feel more like a seminar than a class. I knew, of course, that the kids would find out that Dr. Moore was my uncle. I also knew that it was my job to make that as invisible as possible.

He started by saying, "Let's begin with a basic understanding. We are all writers. If you have written a letter to your grandmother or a note to a boyfriend or girlfriend in class or a book report or a theme for English class you are already a writer. You may aspire to be another Edna Ferber or F. Scott Fitzgerald someday but we must begin by acknowledging that today we are all writers. To do otherwise would imply that there is some artificial gulf or reef that separates us from our dream, and that is not true. Forgive me if I'm wrong but I'm assuming that you're here perhaps for more than one reason but that at least one of them is that some day you'd like to write better than good fiction. I don't think you'd be here if you couldn't already write good fiction so let's get on with the perfection of the almost perfect."

Rich Moore was tweedy in class in chino slacks and corduroy jacket with leather elbow patches. His style also was casual as he stood at a small lectern, roamed around the room, sat on the front of his desk or on the top of one of two steps of the low platform supporting his desk.

Building on the reference to perfection Dr. Moore picked "The Choice," a favorite short poem by the great Irish poet W.B. Yeats. You probably studied him in high school, he said, and know that he was the first Irish writer to receive the Nobel Prize. Since you are, as writers, also artists what he has to say there in "The Choice" may be of interest to you not only as a writing student here but also as you will surely envision yourself some day as an author. Yeats says,

"The intellect of man is forced to choose
Perfection of the life, or of the work."

"What does he mean?" Dr. Rich said. Then, silence for thought.

One of the girls said, "You can have the good life or the good work but not both."

Rich pointed at one of the guys. "You can devote yourself to perfecting yourself or perfecting your art. Whichever, the sacrifice will be greater than the result."

"Think about this," Rich said. "There will be no tests in this course but I would like the great poet's words to influence you in your writing here, to become something you can hear in your lives twenty or thirty years from now. You will be influenced by many writers as you grow and by each other as we read and study your own efforts. But don't forget Yeats as you begin to set the priorities for your lives. And remember also that given a choice, in the end, people always trump paper." I didn't know about the others in the class but I sensed that Rich's last words would need to guide me for a lifetime as a woman if not as a writer.

At the start of the second class Rich said, "This morning I'd like, as I always do, to spend some time on introductions, on getting to know each other. A good class must have at least some fiber of a family. But first I need to call your attention to a new book." He held the book up. "It is *Characters Make your Story* by Maren Elwood. You can get it in the college book store or downtown at Muldoon's Book Store. We will talk about plot and narration and setting and description and dialogue but remember that without characters who seize the imagination your book will fail. People love scenery but mostly they love other people. Like me, you may adore Hemingway, and may he forgive me for this, but his characters seem always to play second fiddle to the forests and the hills and to death and to snows. I wonder sometimes even if he knew how to love women. But we'll deal with Ernest as hero later. Just remember, too, that the Grand Canyon can stir powerful emotions but not the same as

Glenn Miller's 'Moonlight Serenade' if you danced to it with your best girl or guy.

"Now to the character you must always know better than any other—yourself. Who are you? Tell us something about yourself. No formula or design just you."

We didn't go by rows or the alphabet, just by impulse. At first the girls seemed more willing to share. Later the guys got with the program, as they say, and surprisingly revealed more of their insides, more of who they are than did the girls. As with the characters we will create, the most interesting things about our classmates were not where they had been nor what they had done but rather what they thought and felt about life and themselves. Rich seemed pleased with their responses. "You seem to have it," he said. "Emotion is the motion in life, the driving force. One more thing, with regard to your writing: A man is what he does when he has a chance to do something else. Writers write. Thanks for today. My turn next time."

I was disappointed in two things. One was that Uncle Rich, for some reason or another, decided not to share either his background or his feelings about life or his own writing. Maybe later I thought. The second thing was, and I thought about Edie and Dr. Sullivan, the legs. You know how women are. When it comes to clothes, unless they're in the military, they're not going to stick with one thing for very long. The slacks were liberating after high school but, after all, when it comes right down to it pants are a guy thing. So, not all at once but bit by bit, a skirt or dress reappeared. You know how we are about the mature males in the family—dads, uncles, big brothers, even grandpas—a breed apart, so to speak. Apparently not so. Even after he started dating Edie he was still on his perch as Uncle Rich. Is it universal, the male preoccupation with the skirt? What, I thought, about priests and doctors and others of that ilk? At eighteen apparently I had a lot to think about, a lot to learn about everything, especially about men. I'd read a short story once about a women's bridge club. Over the card table the talk turned to the universal topic and one of the women said that her husband would look if a three year old girl stooped over to pick a flower. Yes, I guess I shouldn't have been but I was disappointed for more than one reason in my Uncle Rich. But then, after all, he was a man, I thought, and maybe being a man, like being a woman, was not all that easy. Of course, I was more than confident that Uncle Rich would not develop, as they say, eyes for me.

Generally speaking I took the bus home and back for vacations. Uncle Rich said he wished he could drive me back and forth more often but he had a girlfriend in Joplin which was in the other direction. Her name was Blanche. She taught English in the local high school where they had met and had actually been high school sweethearts.

"Would it be rude of me to ask, after all these years, if your relationship with Blanche was at all personal?"

"As my niece," he said, "it would not be rude. But as your uncle it would be disrespectful to you."

I could only conclude that I'd just been put in my place as courteously as humanly possible.

There were times when Uncle Rich, on his way to St. Louis to see his friends Denise and Roger, offered to drop me off in Cossins. It was on such occasions that Uncle Rich, just the two of us in his car, shared more about himself and especially his ideas about fiction writing. He didn't ask but I vowed to myself that I would not be able to share these moments with my classmates. At first I wondered, also, if he were unprofessionally giving me a fiction lesson advantage over the other students. But then I realized that teachers have aside conversations all the time with colleagues and friends about their work. And after all I was his niece, wasn't I? And after all it was possible that, as it seemed he'd had with Edie, he had a personal interest in me that transcended blood. I didn't really want to dwell on that but, as I had acknowledged before, he was a man. And, I had to admit to myself, I was a woman.

We talked about his writing. He was writing a novel but, in typical fashion, didn't want to discuss it. He surprised me. He said that if Fitzgerald's *This Side of Paradise* was, as a well-known critic had said long ago, a work of genius, then he might well be on his own way to some sort of greatness. He didn't comment on other writings of Fitzgerald and I hadn't read *Paradise* so I thought it best to leave it there but, along with his classroom comment about Hemingway, I thought that these personal comparisons and references might reflect a vanity I didn't expect. Of course, in this case, there were just the two of us so I gave myself the prerogative of feeling somewhat privileged and of hoping that Uncle Rich might be more discreet in class. I wanted to ask him about personal writing habits but we were at the door of my home in Cossins. I asked him if he wanted to come in for coffee or a drink but he said no that he'd better get down the road. I wasn't sure why but I protected my skirt as I left the car.

It was still early. Edie and Dad were at work at the hospital. Mom was in the kitchen fixing dinner. I kissed her on the cheek. She asked why Rich had not come in for awhile. I said that he was on his way to St. Louis to see his friends. I asked Mom if she knew Uncle Rich's girlfriend in Joplin. Mom looked high up on the wall as if trying to picture the girl. Her name is Blanche I said. "I thought it was a buddy in Joplin," she said, "a guy friend. I don't know. I wish he'd get married and settle down. And I don't mean with either of you girls."

"I'm tired, Mom. I think I'll lie down before dinner. Wake me when Dad comes home. I love you."

"Love you, too, Dear."

I got undressed and slipped under the bedspread. I couldn't drop right off so I lay there thinking about life and college and writing and Uncle Rich. I was beginning to understand college and a little more about life. But about Uncle Rich and writing I knew I had a long way to go. In the car I'd asked him about preparation for writing each day. He told me that he wrote early in the morning before his classes and even before breakfast because his head was clearest at that time and because "no one wants you at five in the morning." I asked him about notes and outlines. Notes are essential he'd said. "Outlines are optional. I used outlines for my first two novels and they went nowhere. Kinda' like clothes, a personal choice. Also, I start with the setting and it must be one that you know very well personally—and that is preferable—or one that you have researched thoroughly. But don't get uptight about each day's work. Sort of slide into it. A favorite Irish poet of mine put it this way:

> Only when you sit down to write, do you discover what you want to say. You never know when you are going to arrive.

His name was Paul Muldoon."

"I take it you like the Irish," I said. "First Yeats and now Muldoon."

"I love the Irish. Per capita the most prolific writers in the world. And don't forget your mom and I are Irish." Actually, I had forgotten it and as I drifted off to sleep I thought, "Girl, that makes you Irish. Be nice if that gave you a leg up."

SEVEN

I WAS APPROACHING TWENTY-TWO NOW and would graduate from Drury in the spring. Edie was twenty-seven, working at the hospital and pleased with the small raises she'd had each of her five years there. Dad and Mom were hanging in there, as Edie liked to say. It turned out that Uncle Rich had other talents. He was enough of a carpenter to have helped to build his bungalow in Springfield. I was surprised. I'd read biographies of writers who had also been musicians and artists and even lawyers but not construction workers.

I was also familiar with the advice frequently given to young people who wanted to make careers out of some aspect of the arts to go into teaching first in order to have something solid to fall back on in case the inner Picasso or Edna St. Vincent Millay fails to show up. But either my guardian angel or one of the nine sister Muses of the arts told me that I could do that, could find a safe harbor for my occupational ship but reminded me also that ships were not made for harbors and that my writing harbor might very well mean a long wait for water, in my case for a publisher. So Mom and Dad and I talked it over and they agreed to back my writing career by adding a small writing room off the back porch but Dad said that he'd need Uncle Rich's help. Mom loved me so I was not surprised that she agreed, too, for two reasons: one, that she had had to pass up a musical career as a pianist for financial reasons and, two, that having seen her older daughter express her free spirit by going off to war, she was glad, she said, to help her younger daughter engage in literary conflict at home. While the construction work was going on that summer after graduation, provided Uncle Rich didn't have any summer classes, he would stay in the guest bedroom. I wasn't sure how I felt about that but the work had to be done and the prospect of starting my literary career right out of college at home with Mom and Dad and without the necessity of a job felt like . . . what was that Ink Spots tune? . . . oh, yeah, "I'm Beginning to See the Light."

My writing room, I learned, took more than just carpentry. There were to be two windows and heating ducts to be run. And then electricity for lights and wall plugs and decisions to be made regarding things like whether to use paint or wallpaper and of course a door for privacy and quiet. I had an old portable typewriter but Mom wanted me to have a sturdy standard that wouldn't slide around and, she said, might give me a sense of professionalism. I was happy to agree. And there was carpet to be selected both for additional quiet and added decor. Mom took me shopping for curtains and furniture. We looked at desks and bookcases and while I liked the bookcases I decided to substitute two broad tables for desks so that I would have plenty of horizontal space for notes and collating and a stack of new encyclopedias. I was excited and, as Edie and I had been taught, open with appreciation for what Mom and Dad were doing for me here and now as well as for all they had done over the years, innumerable gifts like feeding and clothing us and, especially, for our educations and our faiths, surely the greatest gifts of all. It was impossible to imagine parents better in every way than those of Edie's and mine. As we had learned to say both at the kitchen and dining room tables, praise God. And, as if all these blessings were not enough, I had an idea for my first novel, a psychological study of a young woman whose life was becoming frustrated and unraveled by her fear, phobia actually, of men. For a long time I couldn't figure out where the idea started, came from. It had been simmering somewhere in the back of my mind even before I left college. Finally it came to me. It was based on a case study from a two-semester course at Drury in abnormal psychology and, more importantly, from watching my sister adjust to civilian life over the past four years.

The guest room was on the first floor but the only bathroom was on the second floor. In order to use the bathroom, therefore, Uncle Rich had to pass my bedroom and Edie's. We'd always kept our doors closed anyway so that was not a problem; Mom had taught us that from the time we were girls. I was getting dressed and had just come back from the bathroom and hung my terry cloth robe on the back of my bedroom door. My door was closed but not clicked shut. I was sitting at my cherry wood vanity inherited from my grandmother and putting on my makeup for the day. I was still in my slip. Out of the corner of my eye I saw the door swing slowly open. Standing in the doorway in his robe was Uncle Rich. He smiled.

"Hi," he said. "Morning."

Startled, I wanted to go to the back of the door for my robe but realized that would only give him a better look. I folded my hands across my chest. "Good morning," I said. "I'm just . . . I'm just getting ready." Of course I didn't know anything about Uncle Rich's tastes in women but as I may have mentioned I was, how should I say, much more ample than my sister and Uncle Rich was not looking at the floor.

"I'm sorry," he said, "just passing through."

My dress was on the bed. I got up, turned away, and reached for it. "Uncle Rich," I said, "maybe you should . . ." I heard the door click shut and when I turned around he was gone.

I don't know if it was unique with me but my figure, the figure some of the girls talked about wanting and most of the guys looked at with wanting, had always—not always but since it appeared—made me uncomfortable. There was a boy at college, David Foster. He was a member of Phi Gamma Delta fraternity, one of the best he said. We had classes together and walked the campus in the snow and in the spring. Between classes we met for coffee in the coffee shop with others, comparing notes and guessing at test questions. Everybody, except maybe me, hated essay question tests so that was always a moaner. David asked me if I'd joined a sorority and I said simply no. I didn't tell him I couldn't afford it.

David and I dated. Movies, a dance or two. We'd kissed. Neither of us was comfortable but the effort was there. Fraternity guys are supposed to be handy (no pun intended) with the girls. David said he was a pledge, a neophyte in the fraternity and I was glad he was also one with me. My passion for writing far exceeded any passion I might have had for David and we drifted apart.

❖❖❖ ❖❖❖ ❖❖❖

It started long before Uncle Rich and Dad finished my new writing room which was a dream come true for me and, I must say, for Mom and Dad and Edie, too. She always wanted the best for me along with the folks. The love was there, in that little town in Missouri, in that old former farm house that had been forced to marry its bride, the growing, maturing, expanding town of Cossins. But more than that the touching was there, had always been there. Oh, our family were not clingers, did not hover over each other but instinctively we knew the value of the touch—and the touch had to include skin. We were huggers, cheek kissers, hand-holders. I remember the story Mom told us during the war about the babies in London during the Nazi blitzkrieg. The hospitals were full of infants for their safety and care, some orphans, some to free parents for military service or for civilian wartime activity. The babies were clean and warm and well fed but after time they started losing weight and becoming lethargic. It was discovered, however, that all of their needs were not being met. The one thing they didn't have was a human touch. So, as they were able, men and women and even teenagers were recruited to come to the wards and spend time each day just holding and rocking the children. Almost at once weight returned with smiles and giggles and energy. How can children grow, Mom asked, and for that matter how can even adults survive emotional atrophy without the touch of hand on skin. How many times I thought had Jesus healed with simply a touch.

As I said it started before the room was finished but we didn't notice it right away. First, Edie asked Doctor Sullivan for a transfer from the men's ward in the acute building to the women's ward. Of course he asked her why. She was hesitant, she told me, even somewhat embarrassed. She said it was the men. He had asked her to sit and for his secretary to close the door. She said her job was physical and often personal and that each day it became harder for her to get in the car and go to work.

"What do you mean by personal?" he said.

Edie looked down at her hands folded in her lap. "You know," she said, "the touching, feeding, even changing of the men."

Doctor Sullivan sucked on his pipe through the flame from a Zippo lighter. "You said you were an army nurse in the war, USS *Mercy* as I recall. You must have seen a lot of blood and body fluids and touched a lot of men, wounded men, dying men. You sent some over the side to an ocean grave, did you not?"

Edie said she blanched, could feel the color drain from her face, the moisture in her armpits. She recrossed her legs. "That's exactly what I don't understand," she said. "I love my job. I felt that, with my army experience and all it was perfect for me." She said that she could feel the tears coming but her purse was on the floor. She said that she wanted to run. Doctor Sullivan offered her a box of tissues.

"Was there anything else?" he said, "anything about men?"

"There was," she said, "actually one thing in particular."

And she told him about Zentsuji Prison on Shikoku Island. As I guess most everyone knows in the telling of an intensely personal story, a story that dives to the guts, like the tales told in the confessional, it is almost impossible to look the listener in the eyes. So, God bless her, she said that she planted her feet together as close to her chair as possible and tried to relate and relive the tea house and the rest of it.

She began with the lie by the Japanese officer that got them into the small boat from the *Mercy*. She told Doctor Sullivan of the torment and martyrdom of those first hours in the Quonset hut. She described the naked embarrassment of one of the nurses in front of stomping and jeering Japanese soldiers, of the murder of their priest, Father Jim, by a frenzied soldier charging out of the bleachers and of the death of that soldier by the officer in charge.

Doctor Sullivan refilled his pipe and removed the Zippo from his vest pocket. Again he slid a box of tissues across his desk. It was warm in the office and he stood and removed his coat and draped it on the back of his chair. Edie said that gave her the chance to do the same, that is take off the jacket to her suit which she had wanted to do almost since the beginning of the interview. In the middle of that move she wanted to stop, not remove her jacket. She was aware immediately that she'd worn a sheer, white nylon blouse under the jacket and under that a lace bra that she was sure the doctor could see through the blouse. She felt, she said, caught in motion, not knowing which way to turn like the squirrel that crosses the road in front of the car only to run back the other way and risk death under the wheels; or the deer at night caught in the glare of the headlights frozen in fear or confused in action. And here was the doctor, a man, watching her, probably unconcerned but, Edie said, not in her mind. She imitated the doctor and placed her jacket over the back of her chair. She sat down and smoothed her skirt and in so doing saw her blouse and through it her bra. What I can see, she thought, so can he and a trickle of perspiration ran down her side and into the band of the bra.

"Is there anything else?" the doctor said.

Edie bit her lip. "Yes," she said, "there is. There is the tea house." For some reason, she said, she thought about losing her top that time at the lake and wished that it was I, Liz', her sister, sitting on the other side of that desk instead of a man.

"Excuse me, Sir, but before I go on I must say that you seem very understanding of all this and I appreciate it."

"You probably don't know, Edith, that I was a sailor in the same war in which your father was a soldier. It gives one, what is the word, compassion? Now what about this tea house?"

"The three of us, the three nurses, were issued into a tea house, I don't know exactly how to describe it except to say that it resembled a rather typical Japanese House as one might imagine from the new novel just out, *The Teahouse of the August Moon* by Vern Sneider.

"In it one reads of rice paper sliding doors thin enough for light to penetrate and probably for one to see through. The room was spacious enough for a massage table in three of the four corners. Japanese music permeated the room and in the fourth corner a young woman in oriental dress played softly on Taiko drums to the rhythms of the music.

"To keep what could rather easily become a long story short, each of us was then issued to one of the three massage tables. Each of us had a geisha to attend us. I assume with a knife that I never saw my geisha slit the back of my clothes dropping them to the floor. I stood naked. Through it all I had the distinct feeling that there were others present, that I was being watched.

"My geisha helped me to lie down on the table, first face down and then on my back. Very gently with delicious-smelling oils she massaged me all over. Doctor, I'm beginning to feel embarrassed, like I'm being too graphic."

"Go ahead, Edith, you're doing fine. I get the picture. Don't worry. I have a wife and three daughters and the only thing I'm feeling is anger at the thought of one of them being caught in your situation. Please go on."

"After she did my back and turned me over she gave me a small cup of tea or saki or something. All I remember after that was her hands on my breasts as she moved down my body. I don't know how much time passed but when I woke up I was still naked and one of the other nurses was standing next to me in a kimono, her hand touching my shoulder. I was groggy. The nurse handed me a kimono. As I sat up to put it on I felt moisture, quite a bit of moisture between my legs. Without further ado, as they say, the three of us in our kimonos made our way to the beach where we were picked up by the launch from the *Mercy*." By then, Edie said, she was covered in perspiration and shaking. The doctor paused to give her time to compose herself. He came around the desk to the back of her chair. He moved her jacket and placed it around her shoulders, standing at her side. He leaned against the desk.

"Is there anything else, Edith?" he said. Edie said later that as a doctor she felt that he already knew there was more and that he also knew what it was.

"The ship's doctor examined me for rape."

"And?"

"There was no sign of rape."

"Penetration?"

"No sign of that, either."

"And the fluids?"

"The fluids. That's the mystery."

I asked my sister if the doctor gave her a definitive answer to her request for a transfer and if he offered an explanation for the presence of the fluids. Doctor Sullivan said that the transfer to the women's ward should not be a problem and that he would discuss it with his personnel director who managed the schedules of all the employees. He asked her, she said, if she'd be willing to talk with a psychiatrist from Jefferson City who was on retainer to the hospital. Edie told him she would. Regarding the mysterious fluids, Edie said, the doctor said he'd be willing to investigate that and that he could already see more than one possible solution. He said also, according to Edie, that as the psychiatrist was also a medical doctor he might be able to shed some light on that. I asked Edie if she felt at all better about things after her interview with Doctor Sullivan.

"Yes," she said, "especially after I left his office."

Switching assignments, Edie said, was no problem. The nurse on the female ward was okay with switching floors. So far, so good, Sis' said. Her psychiatrist, or shrink as she put it, seemed like a nice guy. His name was Doctor Estes and he was good looking and had an easy manner about him. She said she'd wanted to ask Dr. Sullivan about a female psychiatrist but that she hadn't wanted to push her luck since Dr. Sullivan had been so cooperative. Edie said that she hoped the fact that he was a man wouldn't hinder progress on whatever her problem was. She saw him twice a week in the morning before going to work.

Dad was off somewhere. We were sitting in the living room with Mom and her coffee, Edie and her bourbon, and I who had graduated to a nice, sweet, red wine. From where I sat I could look through the open door of my new writing room and smile. Life was good and so were Mom and Edie and I prayed that she knew she had our complete support. It was almost dinner time and I was hungry but Edie was talking about Dr. Estes and I was there for her as if we were twins.

"I was, frankly, surprised," Edie said. "I'd always thought that this psychiatry thing took forever." Now she really had me, I thought. "After only six sessions," Edie said, "he came straight to the point." Mom took a sip of her coffee and I my wine. Oddly, I thought, Edie had not touched her bourbon. She had Mom and me in, as they say, the palm of her hand. We waited. "Dr. Estes says I have androphobia, a fear, a very strong, irrational fear of men. I took a really big, deep breath and asked him if there was a cure. He said no, that there was no cure but that he would try to help me cope with it and without medication if possible and if I was willing."

"How do you feel about that?" Mom said.

Edie took a sip of her drink and looked from Mom to me. "What do you two think?" she said.

Mom looked from me to Edie. "You'll make it," she said. "And Liz' and I and Dad will be in the stands rooting for you all the way." We toasted and hugged as Dad walked into the room. "Something smells awful good," he said. "Let's eat."

As Edie journeyed deeper into her acquaintance with her new friend, if that is an appropriate reference, called androphobia, she wanted to share that education with Mom and Dad and me. However it was not always easy getting the three of us together at the same time. Usually, after Sunday Mass we went home for one of Mom's delicious stew pot dinners or, rarely, to a local eatery in Cossins or, very rarely, to what Mom called a real restaurant in Jefferson City. Today, this Sunday, however, I suggested a picnic in a small park on a hill overlooking our town. There were permanent cooking grills and bench-tables and swings for the little kids but we spread our Irish-Green blanket on the ground. Dad got the cooler with our drinks in it out of the car while us girls laid out the picnic of potato salad, tuna salad, ham sandwiches, and carrot cake. We had our sweaters. Spring was vying with the tail end of winter for control over picnics and convertible drives through the countryside.

Mom had brought a thermos of coffee and Dad and Edie sipped their bourbon and I my wine. We had been fed divinely at Mass and now temporally here. We were full and waited now—as if we'd been told but had not—for Edie to begin. I don't know about Mom and Dad but for some reason I hadn't expected Edie to begin where she did.

"Dr. Estes seems to think that a significant element of my problem comes, or as he says 'emanates' from my time in the prison on Shikoku Island and in the Tea House. He says that androphobia sometimes results from rape, sexual assault other than rape, verbal abuse, or the witnessing of verbal or physical abuse by men against women, especially in the family setting. I told him I could understand the possible trauma resulting from the horror in the barracks that resulted in Father Jim's death but in the Tea House the assault would have had to come from my geisha, a female."

I looked at Dad. He was smoking a cigarette and sipping his Bourbon and studying the few shoots of new grass around the blanket. I wasn't sure just how much of Edie's story he wanted or needed to hear. I wasn't concerned about Mom. Us girls, you know, are pretty tough critters. Like a Van Gogh painting in the Arles countryside, I took in this family pastoral scene as though to permanently sear it into my mind and heart, a Norman Rockwell scene carried surely by every American of halcyon family times burned into our beings like the smell of a roasting chicken or a favorite old sweater. Somehow I knew that this scene, if not its theme, would appear one day in one of my novels.

I was somewhat surprised that Edie could do it but almost without hesitation she moved from part one, the androphobia itself, to part two and, especially with Dad here, the subject of the vaginal fluids in the Tea House. I knew the subject had to be broached in or out of Dad's presence but the topic seemed in such stark contrast to the unsterile warmth of a family picnic that I couldn't at that moment picture how the two would, could meld. In order, I felt, to relieve the delicateness of the conversation Edie moved the role of narrator to Doctor Estes.

"There is a man, a Belgian, a Doctor Tresse who postulates the existence of an organ about three inches upward in the vagina, a Tresse he calls it, I'm sure to claim it as his own, so to speak, that he says approximates the male prostate; in fact he is calling it the female prostate, something heretofore, at least in my medicine, unheard of. After examination of Dr. Tresse's theory, depending on what was in the cup you say the geisha gave you to drink and to the extent to which the geisha's massage may have involved your genitals, it may be possible that the fluids you describe as between your legs when you were awakened by your fellow nurse were your own and not the result of activity by a Japanese soldier or any other male. Therefore, your perfectly valid concern regarding your virginity, if in any way Dr. Tresse is correct may justifiably be laid to rest."

I thought: Don't you just love the way doctors talk? It seems to me that you'd have to go to school for years just to be able to get a handle on the lingo, let alone all the bones, organs, and diseases.

Dad, in his almost perfect but unintentional portrayal of a little bit of Gary Cooper and a little more of Jimmy Stewart, stood up to stretch. "I don't know," he said, "if I'm out of place or out of grace or both but I have to ask a question." I was twenty-two at the time and still a virgin but I hadn't just, as they say, fallen off the cabbage truck. I'd learned a lot from Mom and Edie and a little bit of grain-of-salt stuff from the girls at school so, although I couldn't anticipate Dad's question I thought I was ready for just about anything. I was right about that but wrong in my guess about Dad's question. Mom and I sat on the blanket waiting for lightning but it was just thunder. Dad looked straight at Edie. "What I want to know," he said, "is if Doctor Tresse is claiming that fluids produced by his so-called Tresse gland, or T-spot I think you called it, are the same as the . . ." Dad paused here again. At one time I thought that blushing was the sole property of girls and women but even through the slight stubble on Dad's face I could see just a hint of rose. " . . . well, as the same as semen?"

I don't know what is more than quiet, I suppose maybe very quiet, but whatever, it descended on our little family somewhat like the fog in

Sandburg's poem. Why "semen" I thought. There are many other words in the realm of biology more difficult to say and, even, to envision than that. Dad came back from the car with another pack of cigarettes and joined us on the blanket. Mom had just poured herself some more coffee from the thermos. Edie had just returned from the public restroom. She spoke next. "Yes," she said, "that's what Dr. Estes says that Dr. Tresse says, that the female is capable of producing fluid during the act of making love that is her version of semen but that it is his Tresse spot that makes it possible."

"Only that spot?" Mom said.

"That's what Dr. Estes says Dr. Tresse says," Edie said.

"Mmmm," Mom said. "Learn something new every day, don't we?"

Dad looked at his watch. "Time to hit the road."

Mom picked up the blanket and folded it. She put her arm around Edie. "Hope you feel better, Dear," she said.

Edie didn't say anything but I thought I could read relief in her eyes. I wanted to hug my sister. I wanted to lie down on her bed with her as we had done so often as little girls growing up and just talk, girl talk, talk about boys and clothes and school and what it means to be Catholic and why it seems so much harder than to be Protestant. When we were very young Mom would put us in the tub together and if we were scared at night one of us, usually me because I was younger, would go to the other's bed to snuggle and talk and find relief for whatever we needed relief from, to find what I just saw in Edie's eyes after Mom gave her a hug and said she hoped Sis' felt better. Let's face it, guys are the weaker sex, but let's also be honest and admit that the strings in the hearts of girls are strung tighter and play the more emotional and romantic tune. I wanted to hug my sister and lie on the bed and ask her if she was afraid of anything, of life, of her future, of things like did she think someday she'd be married. But she was twenty-seven now and I was twenty-two and we didn't do that now, couldn't do that now, could we? And then, as we drove back home in the car I wondered about the rush to grow up, to be adults where we could smoke and drink and do our own thing but couldn't lie on the bed together and just talk. I was awfully glad to be a girl, a woman, but at that moment, as I thought I saw girlhood disappearing, I had to admit that, for whatever reason God worked it all out, the guys did have something, too.

It was true, Sis' was twenty-seven and I was twenty-two, but why did it look like I was on my way and she was just beginning, maybe not even beginning but trying to get on the road. After all, she was a nurse and I was trying to become a novelist so, really, who was on the road and who was trying? And yet her career and the war and all she'd been through seemed to have left Edie searching. She went to work every day on the women's ward and kept her appointments with Dr. Estes but something was missing.

And then one day something happened, something that looked a little like the tow truck she needed. She came home for supper but she was not alone. From the living room window I saw them get out of Sis's car and walk to the front door. They were smiling but not holding hands. He was dark and handsome but not tall.

In the living room Edie was smiling. She introduced Danny Landy all around and me as her sister Elizabeth. No one except Mom and Dad had ever called me Elizabeth and I preferred Liz' because I thought it gave me just a touch of the boy that lies in all us girls.

"This is the Ensign Landy that I wrote you about from the *Mercy*," Edie said. "I hope we have an extra plate." Ensign Landy, now, from the civilian clothes I assumed to be Mr. Landy, seemed composed and self-assured but ever so slightly ill at ease. Mom had chicken fricassee, easy to accommodate a guest at the last minute, and mashed potatoes with white gravy and fresh cauliflower. Danny was thin but he didn't eat much. Was it the strange house I wondered or the war still too close or something else? I liked him right away but there was something, something that left me curious.

◈◈◈ ◈◈◈ ◈◈◈

Edie and Danny had been dating on and off for awhile and he was a dinner guest at the house on and off and appreciative and a gentleman always. As I had said I liked him right away but that curiosity had remained. There had been no talk of why Danny was in Cossins besides his interest in Edie until one night after dinner in the living room. Mom and I had finished up in the kitchen and were drying our hands on tea towels. I called to see if Dad or Edie wanted anything. Dad said he wouldn't mind two fingers of Bourbon and Edie said me too. I got my wine and was about to pour Mom some coffee when she said she'd like some of my wine. Dad put the paper down and Edie lighted a cigarette. The scene was ordinary enough but there was that feeling that a shoe was about to drop. There was talk of crops and spring rain and Holy Week and how was everyone doing with their Lenten sacrifice. Then Edie spoke.

"I have a question," she said, "about Danny and it involves all of us. Danny is at the hospital, oddly enough, for the same kinds of things that I'm seeing Dr. Estes for." The three of us perked right up with a how-can-that-be look on our faces. "Oh, I don't mean that," Edie said and chuckled. "Not, of course, that female stuff. Danny was admitted to the hospital for war related emotional problems. I may have told you that Dr. Sullivan spoke of that during my interview with him about my transfer to the women's ward." Mom nodded and Dad looked like he remembered it. Actually, I hadn't remembered so I just waited for Edie to continue. "Danny doesn't need the acute building and he's on outpatient status from the Intake Building so except for his sessions with his psychiatrist he's pretty much on his own." No one else spoke so I waited for the shoe. It came next. "Danny asked me if he could rent a room in the house. I really didn't know what to say so I told him it would be up to the family." She butted one and lit another cigarette. The silence was to be expected. After all, for all these years, except for an occasional overnight or that time Uncle Rich helped Dad with my new writing room there had been just the four of us. You don't have to be the pope to know that people just don't like change, especially very personal change. Dad spoke next.

"Did you tell Danny that we don't have an extra room now that Liz' is home from college?"

"I thought," Edie said, "maybe that little alcove room that Uncle Rich used during the project. It needs a bit of fixing up but since Mom moved all her sewing stuff out for Uncle Rich . . ."

I felt that I had to say something. "I could rearrange my writing room," I said. "Or maybe even move it up to the alcove."

"I don't think that would work," Mom said. "Besides, Liz' has a full time job as a novelist and she needs her private space."

I knew someone had to say it so I waited . . . and waited . . . and finally Dad said it. "Five people and one bathroom?" he said. "Let's play Canasta and think about it."

We thought about it and, mainly I think, because Mom's attitude had always been that there's always room for one more, Danny moved in and began to make the alcove his own. Mom said that they could talk about rent later coming both from her heart and from the idea so prevalent at that time that there was nothing too good for those who had fought the second Great War. After all, she told me one day in the kitchen, we have two recovering soldiers under our roof . . . well, she said one soldier and one sailor but does it make any difference? It did not and I never found out nor did I ask if the subject of rent ever came up again. Apparently, Danny was, at least temporarily, one of the family and I guessed that that made Edie very happy but it didn't show as I thought it might. Now Dad and Edie and Danny went to the hospital together every morning and Mom and I stayed home, I to my novel and Mom to the role she loved as well as hub of our little and loving world.

One Friday night after dinner Dad was reading the *Post-Dispatch*. "Guess what," he said. "Danny Thomas opens for a week at the 'Top O' The Chase.' Let's go dancing."

I don't think I'd ever seen Mom looking more beautiful. She wore a black knit dress with a sharp vee neck. A string of small pearls lay around her neck in color contrast to the dress and in geometric contrast to the vee neck. Mom always followed the church's admonition regarding modesty in dress but tonight was sort of special so she allowed maybe an inch or two of cleavage. Her dark hair was done in a page boy, a style that nicely framed her oval face and that I'd heard Dad say made her look sexy. Two tiny, pearl earrings clung to the lobes of her ears. I thought she wore "White Shoulders" but I wasn't sure. I didn't have the usual scent powers given to most women. At any rate Mom looked lovely and, yes, I must admit, sexy. She was, as they say, all dressed up to go dancing or, as the popular song said, dreaming.

The men, of course, wore their suits. I was just getting used to Danny out of uniform but he had good taste and the blue suit was as close to navy as one could get. Dad didn't dress up often except for church but he had the build and the taste to look comfortable as well as smart. I was a bit giddy for the occasion as well as very proud of my whole family. I wore a black skirt and a tailored white blouse, the blouse, as usual, to minimize my full bust.

The club at the top of the Chase was beautifully but tastefully appointed, nothing garish. We had a table just off the dance floor. The waiter took our drink order. I had a rum and Coke for a change. Dad said we'd wait awhile to order food and we settled down to watch the band warm up for the young, new hit who called himself Danny Thomas. Dad had said earlier that this was to be his treat. Things looked good; in fact, except for my sister's coming home, my new writing room, and Danny Landy's arrival things hadn't looked this good for a long time. Ecstatic may not have been the perfect word but it was close.

The band started playing for dancing quite awhile before Danny's first show. He was making his way through radio and into television, starting as a singer and comedian. We learned from a card on our table that he was of Lebanese extraction, grew up selling newspapers at ten, and was a devout Roman Catholic. We learned later that he was also very funny and more than a passable singer. The band was excellent but local rather than one he travelled with.

Mom and Dad danced first and were, I thought, quite good. Edie and Danny hung back at first, uneasy I guessed that I'd be left sitting by myself. I shooed them off and for two people I figured had never danced together before did well. The band played its version of Glenn Miller's "Moonlight Serenade" and "In the Mood." Mom and Dad came back and he asked me to dance but I'd developed a bothersome toothache so I begged off and swished the rum and Coke through my teeth. Edie and Danny stayed on the floor until the band stopped playing as a sign that the other Danny was about to appear. We were ready, as this kind of night out was uncommon for the Endsley family.

The word "consummate" means perfect, complete in every way. As such, the question regarding its use may well be asked: must its use be restricted to experts in the field in question? In other words may the use of the word be open to so-called amateurs in any given area of endeavor.

For example, may the average baseball fan in the stands fairly use the term "consummate" to describe a player or must the word be reserved for professional commentators who've spent whole careers honing skills of evaluation.

I don't know. And I'm forever-and-a-day away from being an expert on anything, especially music, and more especially popular music. But I'm going to say it anyway: Danny Thomas that night was a consummate performer. I wouldn't say handsome in the Hollywood tall, dark, and handsome, Cary Grant model but manly, smooth, warm, engaging. When he sang he sang to me alone, when he was funny he opened his arms and his heart to the entire room and, in so doing held all sixty or seventy of us in—I don't want to say it but I will—the palm of his hand. (At the moment that I had that thought, as a writer, I was grateful to God that I was not covering the event for my newspaper. I could have seen my editor roll his eyes, ball my copy up in his hand and toss it in the basket.)

Hackneyed or not the palm of his hand is where Danny Thomas that evening held all of us in a magic surpassing that of Harry Houdini. I could see perhaps for the first time, for I was still very young, the subtle power of a man. Between songs and laughs in the presence of Danny Thomas I became more of a woman. It may not have been the *Titanic* but it was definitely a night to remember.

I was tired. It must have been close to two in the morning. In the back seat of Dad's car I was on the left, Edie in the middle, and Danny

Landy on her right. That order was established by Danny's holding open the car door for us. I was sleepy. I'd had three drinks and, in spite of a lovely and expensive dinner that, for me, was probably one too many. I noticed, as I let my head drop onto Edie's shoulder, that she and Danny were holding hands. That shouldn't have surprised me and it didn't, but what did surprise me was Danny's hand in my hair as I fell asleep.

EIGHT

NINETEEN FIFTY-TWO HAD BEEN A good year. Dwight Eisenhower was elected President. Dad liked him, he said, because after the campaign Dad saw a man of quiet strength, one who'd been graced with the genius to bring victory and peace to the European continent. Having spent time on the *Mercy* Edie saw "Ike" as a new style leader, one who is willing, as is the captain of a ship, to let the crew or, in this case, the people govern. She said that the captain is the least visible man on the ship, of the crew if that can be said of the captain. And Mom kicked in with her idea that Eisenhower was a man who, as a general, would not lead from behind but would emphasize government not only of and for the people but *by* the people. "I may never have been in the army," she said, "but it seems to me that a good general, like a good teacher or a good priest should get out of the way and let the troops, so to speak, get the job done. And that includes the President." Mom had a mind of her own and knew how and when to speak it.

Danny Landy brought up General MacArthur who had been to the Pacific Theater what Ike had been to the European Theater. Like Edie, Danny had done his time on the other side of the world helping to put down the Japanese dream, or nightmare, of turning the Pacific Ocean into that small country's front yard swimming hole.

Danny moved out and into an apartment. He'd landed a job at a local engineer/architecture firm and said he wanted to be closer to work. Actually, I think he'd felt he'd been crowding us but he was probably alone in that. He was still working with his psychiatrist at the hospital as an outpatient and dating Edie although for some reason their arrangement didn't seem conventional.

Of course, Edie and Dad were still at their posts at the hospital and Mom was running the ship. I was at work on my novel based loosely on the life of Marjorie Kinnan Rawlings, a woman I'd admired since childhood and whose life should be read by every girl in the country.

As I said, nineteen fifty-two was a good year for many reasons but mainly for the end of the war, the election of Ike, the fact that our family was rockin' along, and that Edie and Danny had survived the war, or so it seemed. That question, about surviving the war for Edie and Danny, remained for me and I think for Mom and Dad, wrapped somewhere in the clouds of our minds. I knew little really about the complexity of Danny's illness but from what Edie told me about her work with Dr. Estes, a major part of Edie's androphobia came from being embarrassed by one's own actions. Of course, I didn't know everything about my sister's life experiences, everywhere she'd been, everything she'd done, and it was none of my business, sister or no sister, but the experience in the tea house, if Edie considered that experience a result of her own actions, might certainly qualify as humiliation. Projecting myself onto Edie's life or, as they say, putting myself in her place, I found it hard to imagine that she had not been forced or at least coerced into a situation that left her wondering or even questioning seriously if she had lost her virginity. In spite of my youth and lack of medical knowledge, I sensed that both Danny and Edie faced trips down a long road.

And I was not without my own problems. It apparently had been growing for some time and I was not aware of it. I was seven years older than when this story began, twenty-three, had done college, as they say, and was living a dream that began when I was seven or eight years old, my dream of writing, of becoming a novelist. My health was good and how many twenty-three-year-olds worry about their health anyway. I didn't have a boyfriend although I did see David Foster from Springfield occasionally. He was going into medicine so that probably wasn't going anywhere. I was no longer concerned about Uncle Rich, either for Edie or myself, especially since his girlfriend, Blanche, whom we had never met, was rumored actually to be a Bradley. So, as I sat at my new typewriter one morning, I asked myself: girl, what's the matter? I had a hard time admitting it then and an even more difficult time writing about it now. I cringed. I was jealous of Edie, jealous of my own sister, who was my flesh and blood, my best friend, someone who if it were not out of the natural order I could have and would have spent my life with. And worst of all it was for the worst possible reason: I realized that I had become envious of her because of all the attention she'd gotten since coming home from the war. And, to add to that, now there was Danny who pulled not only his own share of celebrity but, it seemed, pulled Edie and me apart.

I decided to talk with our priest about all this so that I could live comfortably with my sister, myself, and especially with my God for I knew that the God who'd given me the gift of words could as well take that gift away. Father explained that jealousy was a common enough human failing and more often than not of those, say friends and family, that we are closest to. He said that God has gifted us all with talents and treasures and that we must discover our own and use them while leaving those of others to themselves. As it was a conversation rather than a confession he ended with a blessing and a reminder that we must first forgive ourselves and that there is no love without forgiveness, "Please do not forget," Father said, "the greatest gift of love was given from the Cross and it was given with a prayer for forgiveness." I went home to my novel with a cleaner if not pure heart. I wanted to lie on the bed with Edie, hold her hand, kiss her, and share the contents of my heart but she and Danny and Dad were at the hospital. Mom asked me where I had been and I told her but I couldn't ask her to lie on the bed with me and talk. We were as close as a Mom and daughter could possibly be but we were not sisters.

My novel was going pretty well. Mom had asked me why I hadn't begun with the short story, reminding me that when Edie started running at school the mile was first followed by the cross county three mile and later into road races. She was right of course and I told her that I'd given that a lot of thought all through college and that I realized that many of the big boys and girls, so to speak, had begun with the short story including Faulkner and Hemingway and one of my female favorites, Eudora Welty. I knew that my vistas of life were not the broadest and also that most endeavors require some sort of workup or preliminary as might be exemplified by a basic training or boot camp in the military, but I had not dreamed of becoming a great short story writer. Dreams are the everything of life, the sine qua non if one doesn't mind the Latin. And that is why, when Edie first came home and seemed rudderless as I'm sure so many of our warriors did, and in spite of my immaturity, I suggested she find an anchor and that that anchor not be a person or even a job or career but perhaps the use of some God-given talent that, along of course with her faith, would sustain her when and if the world might leave her feeling adrift. Edie was, of course, a nurse. She had used her skills well in the Second Great War and was continuing to serve in the State Hospital, but I sensed, maybe just because it was a career that it might never sustain her as an anchor in life. In reading the lives of the notable artists, composers, scientists, builders, writers, and philanthropists one sees beyond their arts, or perhaps *in* their arts, an anchor that strengthens them not only in their work but to the point that, having lost all else, they find it possible to continue. This might be genius but, as it is possible to find in even the meager life, may not be, may be simply the David in all of us when faced with a Goliath.

NINE

I T WAS THE MOST HORRIBLE thing that ever happened to me. Shakespeare said that comparisons are odious which, of course, is not the same as, and infinitely worse than, odorous. The former coming closer to detestable, the latter simply to offensive. What happened to me, and to the family and to God only knows how many other people around the world was the death of my father, the most detestable thing, other, of course, than the premature death of my mom or my sister that I can imagine. I'm deliberately avoiding, or delaying, the details because, of course, death must come to us all and not just to Willa Cather's archbishop but we pray (if we ever actually allow ourselves to pray about death at all) that the death of our loved ones and even those we don't know personally will come naturally and painlessly.

It was not so with Dad. Naturally and painlessly may be thought of as without shock. There is the classic story of the man who survives the beach at Normandy and comes home to die under the wheels of the bus he used to take to work. It was not so with Dad.

All state hospitals for the mentally ill have patients designated as trusties, those patients who have demonstrated a level of trust to allow them to function in special capacities of service within the institution. For example, Edie told me about a trusty on the men's ward when she worked there who assisted the nurse and the male nurse attendant with hygienic cleanup duties and the removal of dead patients to the morgue in the basement.

The man who killed my dad was such a man, a trusty. I don't know his name, don't want to know his name. I refused to read the account in the local paper and, although I didn't want to I forced myself to sit with Mom and Sis and Uncle Rich and close friends in our living room and hear the story.

This man, the man who killed my father, the best man who ever lived, the man who'd been by my side forever, the man who bought me my first training pants and, when Mom was sick in bed, my first training bra, the strongest, quietest man, this murderer was such a trusty. His job, apparently for a long time, was serving mashed potatoes on the food line in the hospital cafeteria. He had been entrusted with a long-handled stainless steel spoon. That was the only utensil he was allowed to have: no forks, no knives, no spatulas, only the spoon. Along with other trusties who served on the line, he was required to turn the spoon in at the supervisor's desk at the end of the line when the meal was over.

Somebody screwed up. Horribly. Somehow the man, along with some others, was ushered back to his ward room in routine procedure carrying the spoon tucked into his pants. Somehow he managed to sharpen the handle end of the spoon into a point. Dad moved along the line and stopped at the mashed potatoes. The man placed a spoonful of potatoes on Dad's tray, turned the spoon around, and stabbed Dad in the chest with the other end, the sharp end. Dad dropped to the floor. In the pandemonium that followed the first concern was the man with the homemade knife. Dad lay on the floor, bleeding, dying. And that's where he stayed, actually where he died. They took him to the acute building but it was too late. The man who killed him was roughed up, but there could be no charges, no trial, no conviction: the man was mentally ill. Of course he was no longer a trusty on the food line or anywhere else. And my father was no longer an employee of the State Hospital. He had acquired a new residence and his wife and daughters had been altered forever.

Edie had started smoking more and the three of us had begun drinking more. A pall had descended over our once warm and beautiful sanctuary. Of course Mom, strong, hub-of-our-world-Mom tried valiantly to carry on. She failed. Edie could no longer work at the hospital so she quit her job. I covered my black Royal with its black cover and my new writing room gathered dust. Oddly there were few tears, at least in moments we shared in the dining room or living room. I don't know why but I guessed that mine was not the only wet pillowcase in the morning. The worst parts were the lethargy, the inertia, the constant pain in the chest. No, the worst part was Dad. Dad was somewhere else, someplace we could not go but in our hearts wanted to. I don't know how much boys cry out in pain at the loss of a mom but I'm a girl. My mom is the heart of our family. My dad was a god to me. First, he was a man and I think maybe that my father was, in the most appropriate way, my first man, the man, the template for the man with whom I might spend my life, a man I hadn't found yet and now didn't know if I ever wanted to find. From what I've read I know that there are what they call Mamma's Boys but I'm not sure that the male makeup allows them to see their mothers as wife surrogates, at least in an almost intimate sense.

Our stock is not one of moan and wail. Our stock tells us things like "Keep a stiff upper lip," and "Carry on." I know that applies as advice in innumerable life situations. I don't know about war and decided not to ask my sister about it and I know what I have to do as a member of my stock but I'm still not sure whether wailing wins out over stiff upper lips. Edie quit seeing Dr. Estes but not before he suggested that the three of us seek some counseling. He didn't suggest himself and I figured that might come from professional restraint.

Just when we shouldn't draw back we did, we stopped going to Mass, stopped really going anywhere that was not necessary for survival like the store and the garage. Then, at dinner one night while we held hands and said the blessing over dinner, Mom asked the Lord to take us back home to his House, to his Church, the only place really necessary for our survival. And we did. And gradually things got better and we said to ourselves and to each other why are we surprised. There was only one food, we knew, that could sustain us in the face of such things as war and death and that food was not in a grocery store. And, most of all, we knew that that was what Dad would have wanted most for his girls, as he always called us, his girls. Even Jesus couldn't stop my tears.

Then one night, Mom had gone to a Ladies Guild meeting at church, Edie said she needed to talk. We sat on the front porch, Edie with her Bourbon and cigarettes, I with my wine. I'd given up smoking for Dad but didn't know it at that time.

Danny wanted to talk, Edie said. I said fine. He said where. I said the bench under the tree near Dad's grave. He said okay. It was a spring afternoon. The breeze was soft and lovely and so was the headstone. Mom said it was more than she could afford but I told Danny that I chipped in. The wording was simple: Roy Endsley followed by dates, followed by "Husband, Father, Catholic, Ambulance Driver, France, W W I, Servant of God and Family." Actually, I told Danny, he was a lot more than all that but the stones are all sized and they charge for each letter. Besides, I said, Dad would have been embarrassed by more, plain, conservative gentleman that he was.

I think, Sis, that Danny could see me starting to tear up so he took my hand. He removed the hanky from it and touched it to each eye. I kissed him on the cheek. "Go ahead," Danny, I said.

He began. "I did move out because I thought I might be crowding the house, although that all came from me and not from you and the folks. But the larger reason was us."

I think, Sis, that I sensed what was coming and I almost wanted him to stop but I knew that, after the war and the hospital and Dad, pain was inevitable so I let him continue, strangely wanted him to continue.

"You remember," Danny said, "after the Tea House and your physical exams and all that we were given passes in Hawaii. It was so exciting and romantic that I don't even remember the name of the hotel but I will never forget that night on Waikiki Beach, the sand under and the soft waves lapping our almost naked bodies."

"Liz'," I shuddered. "I was so much in love, we were so much in love. I wasn't sure where Danny was going but I found out when he mentioned the night on the balcony. In two nights on a honeymoon that didn't belong to us I was no longer a virgin. Danny was good, tender, knew exactly what to do without pushing. I didn't ask him how he knew, didn't want to spoil anything. We returned to the *Mercy* and were discharged at Treasure Island under the bridge in San Francisco. I hadn't seen him again until he showed up at the hospital. Of course, we wrote for awhile but that didn't last either.

"Then I come home to discover that I have this abnormal fear of men, androphobia, and have to relive the Tea House and maybe the blood and guts of the *Mercy* and wonder what else might have contributed to the problem. Danny? For example?

"I suppose to stall the conversation I asked him if he was related to the great Australian distance runner, John Landy, the second man to break the four-minute mile. He said no, not that he knew of. Then he continued.

"You know, Hon'," he said to Edie, "there was only one other time, for either of us I hope, that afternoon while I was living in the house and the folks had all gone somewhere. Remember? It was in your room. And that's part of, maybe all of, the reason I moved out. I still want you, still need you but I sense that things have changed."

Yes, Sis, I thought, things have changed and in ways not even you know yet.

"Now that things have started to settle down," Danny said, "you know now that you're no longer at the hospital and your dad and all, maybe we could take some time off and go to Chicago. The folks have a little place near Lake Geneva. We could rest up and I could show you the sights."

"What about our psych' work at the hospital?" Edie said.

"Either we can take a break," Danny said, "or I'm sure we can have the paper work sent up. We need to be together, Edie."

"Sis," Edie said, "I felt a tightness in my chest unlike anything since Dad died. I've never felt so torn, the pain was excruciating. If I have to go away somewhere could you explain to Danny? I don't think I can."

"Go away, Edie, where? What do you mean?"

TEN

IT HAD BEEN ALMOST THREE years since Dad was murdered. The pall had lifted gradually, something like the flowers that open in time-lapse films. The lift was in its own way a beautiful thing, a lovely thing but there is a price to pay even for beauty it seems and the lifting of the pall opened the world up again to us all. Dad had resigned and we allowed him to resign to the mystery of his new place, that place we didn't want to think about but had always to return to in our minds in order to find balance in our lives.

Mom had taken Dr. Estes up on his suggestion that we could all profit from some therapy. Of course, she went alone because that's the way it's done. I hadn't got there yet. Then one afternoon I came out of my writing room and Dr. Estes and Mom were sitting in the living room apparently having a drink before dinner. Mom introduced us. He seemed like a nice man, about Dad's age but not from the First War. Conversation revealed that he had applied for return to service near the end of World War II when the government was offering reenlistments with commissions to veterans of the war against the kaiser regardless of rank from that war. These were men in their late forties and fifties. In the vein of Dr. Sullivan Dr. Estes was not accepted because of his position at the hospital. Except for the fact that he was more studious, more academic, he reminded me of Dad.

In the conversation I picked up on entering the room Mom and the doctor were discussing either the possibility of taking a cruise or of a long weekend at the lake, at Chateau-Thierry. My first reaction was that someone was treading on sacred ground. Then I looked at Mom in a dress I'd seen so many times, one I think Dad had bought for her and I told myself to get over it, in effect to get a life not only for myself but to help if I could in Mom's flower opening. I got my wine and joined them. Mom said we were having fish frozen from the lake. That sounded good. I could see Dad catching them, although those fish, though lasting a good while were long gone. I wasn't ready to ask whether or if they were going on a cruise or to the lake, but I did know that if they went to the lake I didn't want to be invited and wouldn't go if I had been. The subject of Mom's therapy didn't come up, as I knew it couldn't, shouldn't, so I didn't say anything but in my heart I was glad she was moving on. What good is a flower that never opens I thought? I asked Mom where Edie was but either she didn't know or didn't want to say. Edie had become more withdrawn lately, even somewhat reclusive. She was out of town sometimes but I didn't ask Mom where. Maybe Mom didn't know, or was giving her older daughter some space. That was okay. That was what we all needed. The fish was good. The second glass of wine was better. I'd found a taste for chardonnay and was told it went better with fish and chicken. I couldn't see the difference.

Over dinner Mom said that Danny had gone home to Chicago to spend time with his family. Dr. Estes didn't comment. He knew Danny and may also have known something about his relationship with Edie.

Uncle Rich was nowhere to be seen. I wasn't comfortable with talk that he may be homosexual but again we all had to move on, didn't we and it's awfully hard to move in two directions at the same time.

I'd pretty much gotten over the misplaced jealousy of Edie's heroic return from the war, concentrating on my writing. Then one day there was a knock on the door and Edie came in without an invitation, something she hadn't done since we were kids. Without saying a word she took my hand and led me to her room. She told me to lie down on her bed and she lay down next to me. She took my hand and held it between us. I had no idea what was going on.

We lay there together, dressed, as we had as little girls all those years ago. Sisters. How powerful, how beautiful, how personal and intimate. We had done this as a way of communion, as a way of intimacy to try to understand each other beyond words. I had lain here by myself, on her bed, to pray for her during the war and to ask her to pray for me and Mom and Dad. I could hear her breathing, see her chest moving up and down so slightly. I loved this girl beyond everything and prayed there and then for her recovery for, as I remembered asking her to do right after she came home, to find an anchor for her life and, as I recall, to find an anchor that was not a person, an anchor that would not desert her when her world went away. I'd found mine in writing, in fulfilling a dream that I felt sure no one could take away from me. I wanted her to have one, too.

She squeezed my hand softly and put it to her lips to kiss it. "I have two things to say," she said, "and then I must go away. First, not long after you got your writing room fixed up Mom asked me to help her clean house. I don't know where you were nor why I wasn't at the hospital but I started in your room. I saw your manuscript next to the typewriter and thought it looked too thick for the time you'd been working. I dusted around your desk but my eyes kept returning to the manuscript, the one about Rawlings, the writer in Florida. Then I saw a piece of yellow paper from a legal pad sticking out from the middle of your manuscript. I felt nosy and probably should have minded my own business but I lifted the Rawlings' manuscript and set it aside. I read the first and the second and third pages of the second manuscript and dropped to the bed in horror."

Of course, now I knew where this was going and I cringed. Edie was never supposed to see this, the second manuscript. I'd started it out of jealousy and envy. Now she was telling me that she had to go away somewhere and the pain in my chest told me that we might not part friends. I was horrified. She still held my hand but now I could feel my palm start to sweat. I could feel a drop start under my arm and run down my side. I turned to look at Edie. She stared straight ahead.

"How could you?" she said. "I thought you loved me."

My heart started beating faster. I squeezed her hand.

"You say you were jealous, envious, when I came home from the Pacific, the older sister, the glory girl. Then you learned that I'd come home not quite all in one piece, didn't you? Came home with a serious problem. Did that make you feel better, Liz, make you feel that maybe the distance between us that had never been there before brought me down a little, took some of the gilt off that ruptured duck I wore on my collar?"

I started to cry, actually sobbing. What could I say? Where could I run to? I was on that bed next to my sister, a bed I'd thought of growing up as a bonding bed, a bed I'd always thought of as a place where my sister helped me grow up. And I had probably destroyed her and if not her our relationship. At that moment I wanted to be anywhere but there—but I couldn't run, I was trapped.

I started to say something. Edie put her arm around me. I turned toward her and felt my face against her breast. Was this an Armageddon, I thought, a futile, final conflict between sisters where there had never been one? Edie kissed my forehead. This was probably the closest physically that we had ever been and I'd never felt so alone, so pained, and it was all my fault, my childish fault.

"Kiss me," she said. I looked up at her. She brought her lips to mine and we kissed, softly, sister-tenderly, with love but without passion. Once again, for the first time since I was a baby, I was in my mother's arms and swept over by security.

"I forgive you," Edie said. And then again softly, "I forgive you."

What is deeper, more powerful than those three words, I thought? My sister looked down at the top of my head. She smoothed my tangled hair with her hand. I could hear and feel the steady beat of her heart through her chest against my face. And then, almost as from a cross she forgave me for such a sin of personal invasion. I didn't know if I should ever feel such love again from anyone. I raised my face to hers. "You said you had two things to say," I said.

"Yes," she said, "two things." She drew me closer to her as if afraid of something. I'd never been this close to a man but I felt sure that, although the intimacy would surely be different, it could not be stronger. "We'll never do this again, Sis', never lie on this bed again together as we have since childhood. You're grown now and your strength must come from the Lord and from someone you don't know now. I am going away. When I came home we talked and you told me I should find an anchor, do you remember? And you said that the anchor should not, must not be a person but something that will see me through the tough times and will not desert me. I think you meant something like your writing."

I was quiet for a moment, thinking, remembering. "Yes," I said, "I do remember that it was about my novels."

"I think I've found my anchor, Liz, but I'm afraid it is a person and not an object, not purely a talent."

"Danny?" I said.

Edie chuckled. "No, not Danny, but it is a man. Liz, I want to be a nun, to serve the God who died for us on the Cross. I've been gone, travelling, visiting various orders."

I was shocked but I don't know why. Edie had always been somewhat ethereal and I thought about Rima the jungle girl in W.H. Hudson's novel, *Green Mansions*. Edie, like Rima, was sylph-like and built more for the flowers than for the hard work aboard the *Mercy*. "Have you found one?" I said, "an order, or is it the other way around, do they find you? What's the process, how do you go about it? Have you told Mom?"

"I love you for your interest, Sis. I guess it's a bit like trolling for a college, the right college. I really like the Sisters of Mercy. They're a nursing order. I was hoping you'd be with me when I tell Mom."

◇◇◇ ◇◇◇ ◇◇◇

As I said, Danny Landy had gone home to Chicago to spend time with his family. Danny, I guess, like Edie and the millions of other returning veterans needed to reconnect with everyone, to find old anchors or new ones for the next parts of their journeys. According to Danny's letter to Mom—he had written her to Edie because, he said, Edie was galavanting around the country doing something and he couldn't keep up with her—his family lived, as most Chicagoans did, in apartments. Theirs, he said was a large but modest flat on Albion Avenue a half block west of Sheridan Road and another block from Lake Michigan. Maybe less than a mile south of Albion on the lake lay Loyola University.

Danny said he'd spent time walking on the beach and on Sheridan Road, talking with his family and, for some reason going to an occasional Mass. His uncle was a lawyer and, after all was said and done and too many movies at the Granada Theater and too much poker and beer with the family he'd decided to apply to law school at Loyola. Loyola was, he said, a Catholic school and he was not Catholic but they accepted him and from his letter it was clear that he was very happy.

He asked Mom to give his love to me and, of course, to Edie when and if she came home. And Edie had come home and we had lain on that bed together in a final closeness that rivaled Valhala in its pain and beauty. And after which we had tracked Mom down wiping her hands on her apron in the kitchen and humming a phrase from Frank's new record, "Try a Little Tenderness." Mom and Dad had loved Frank and had found time often to dance in the large kitchen. Now Mom was humming alone and there was no more dancing but Edie took her by the waist and spun her around and hummed the tune with her. Mom smiled as they twirled until I saw the tears in her eyes. At that I joined them arms around waists and we slid slowly across the floor as we had when we were all much younger and Dad would stand in the doorway and smile. The song was ended and the needle stuck in the grooves at the middle near the little hole but as another song says the melody lingered on. We hugged and kissed on cheeks until we broke apart laughing and Edie said we needed to talk; "we" she said, which of course pleased me as included.

It was late afternoon. We got our drinks—Mom coffee, I my wine, and for the first time that I could remember, Edie had tea. We went into the living room still smiling from the dancing and the sisterhood,

Mom huffing a little from the exercise. It reminded me that despite the biology present we were, at least to God, sisters, his children, for they say that God does not know time, does not have time in spite of having created it. The female mystique: women, related or not but especially when blood is present. Artists have painted this mystery and composers have written music for it but no one really knows what it is, knows why it exists even through jealousy and rancor. There is a female Catholic saint, I think it was Catherine of Siena, who came close by linking this mystique, loosely of course, to the case of women's reproductive systems being for all practical purposes internal. I think Saint Catherine, in this observation, was trying to propose purity, chastity, and in so doing was telling women that the riches of God had given them reside in their hearts and gave them a superiority that men could never know. I don't know, probably can't know ever about Saint Catherine and her genius but I do know that, despite life with all its slings and arrows, life lives most fully, most completely in the mystery known as woman. How different, I thought, would the conversation we were about to have about Edie be, if the subjects were men.

Edie lighted a cigarette and Mom followed. I had abandoned them. I knew that the picture of the writer, even Rawlings, crouched over the typewriter, smoke curling overhead, was supposed to be romantic but the smell that lasted turned me off.

It seemed strange, the three of us in the living room about to begin a discussion, a serious discussion, without Dad. I couldn't remember such a time before. Oh, there might have been talks about girl-type things without him but even at that Dad had been such a visceral part, member, of our family that despite the striking and obvious differences between Dad and us girls I had, without design or caring, come to see my dad as almost androgynous, as a guy who could float back and forth between family roles, a man referred to by Robert Whittington as a "man for all seasons."

We sometimes hear people say of someone that there is nothing he or she can't do. Dad could dabble in just about anything: what do they say? "jack of all trades, master of none." I don't know where he got it and it doesn't really matter but Dad was a master of the gifts of husband and father. Men like to do their own things but too often, it seems, those things turn up late in life as inconsequential when they realize they had a wife and children they never got to know. Cornelius Whurr, a man I'd never heard of, wrote "What lasting joys the man attend/Who has a polished female friend." I don't know about "polished" but in Mom and Edie and me Dad had three female friends without rival.

I heard a priest say one time that the only goal of parents is to get their children into heaven. Dad's parents did it for him. I can only pray that he did it, along with Mom of course, for us.

We were talking about life one time, just Dad and me, and he told me that at the Indianapolis 500 the race begins when the announcer says, "Gentlemen, start your engines." Dad patted me on the knee. "That," he said, "pretty much sums up all we know about men." I took his arm as he started to get up. He looked down at me. "Not," I said, "not this man."

I said earlier the three of us, Mom and Edie and me. Actually there were four of us—Dad's chair, that man-type chair, was still there; it was just empty.

This old house, our house where Dad and Mom and Edie and I had forged a family together was once, Mom had told me, a farmhouse. But the town had moved in on it or more accurately, out on it until a small pasture across the road and a vacant silo near a hill in the back were all that remained of once countrified Cossins. Oh, I knew about Ellis Island and the wonderful ethnic floods that washed ashore in New York to build the skyscrapers and hawk their wares on Delancey Street. But I knew also of the farm boys and girls who would go, went, from here, from Cossins and a hundred thousand towns like her to France twice to preserve silos and farmhouses and a Cossins way of life. Here were American physical and spiritual muscle of a special kind, the kind we sang about in school and church as "America the Beautiful" found its way into our bones and blood.

The living room I guess was the special room. We talked around meals at the kitchen and dining room tables but those conversations were what Dad would have called lightweight. Like school and work and the new curtains in the bedroom. But when it came to something like tonight, as Mr. Sullivan would say, something really big, it was the living room.

Our living room was not the kind you sometimes find in houses in town that are set aside for special occasions none of which are special enough to warrant use of the room. I struggle to find the words, the description. It smelled softly like a bit of linseed oil and O-Cedar. The dark wood was still dark. The chandelier had been replaced with the most expensive ceiling fan Dad could find either in town or in a catalogue. He thought a chandelier was a bit too pretentious and was either never used or robbed the room of warmth.

Two large windows between the entranceway and the fireplace at the north end faced south across the meadow on the other side of the road. Two smaller windows flanked the fireplace at the west end of the room. A couch faced the fireplace from the middle of the room and two chairs faced the couch and flanked the fireplace. Edie and I sat on the couch. Mom sat on one of the chairs. The other was Dad's. It was a nice room, a room where we liked to spend time, a room that held Christmas and before that at Thanksgiving, a brandy and maybe one of Dad's cigars.

Edie spoke first. "I've been doing some travelling."

Mom said, "We've missed you. Especially Danny. He went home to Chicago for awhile."

"I got a letter," I said. "He says he's been accepted at Loyola Law, says he'll be living with his folks. It's only a few blocks away he says. I think I could feel the pain in what he feels is his loss of you, Edie."

It grew quiet. The smoke from Mom's cigarette climbed toward the high ceiling, designed to trap the hot air of summer.

Edie folded her hands in her lap. I waited. I wanted to hug her. "Mom," she said, "I want to become a nun."

I had all kinds of things I wanted to say but this was not my moment. This was, so to speak, a moment of truth between my sister and my mom. Not ten feet away sat the woman who had carried Edie and me in her womb. I looked at her waist. From there thirty years ago had emerged the grown woman who sat next to me on the couch. What must be going through that woman's mind I wondered: the nursing, the diapers, the bows in the hair, first grade, high school, the war, the damage the war had done, and now this. Surely, Mom could not be unhappy. Our faith called for this, actually cried out for this. No son to offer God in the priesthood but a wonderful daughter to follow in the foot steps of Mary. I waited. The silence produced a soft ringing in my ears. As I guess all of us do Edie had her own scent. Sitting with our thighs almost touching I could smell it, almost feel it. Again I waited. Mom had to say something. Outside a car passed, the engine a soft hum, probably an older person I thought. I thought of Dad. He should be here, shouldn't he? He was always here for these important times wasn't he? But once again now Mom had to do for both of them.

Mom got up from her chair and walked to us. She knelt in front of Edie as I could picture her doing in the confessional. She took Edie's hands in hers and kissed them. "I am so happy, Dear," she said. "And I know Dad is happy."

I don't know how but somehow I knew what Edie would say next and she did.

"Grandchildren?" she said.

Mom looked into Edie's eyes, smiled, and said, "Jesus will give us grandchildren of another kind through your love and devotion to Him just as priests receive huge families through their devoted celibacy as Fathers, heavenly Fathers. You've made me very happy, Edie, and tonight in bed I will have a long talk with your father. Now get some wine and we will celebrate as Christ and his Mother celebrated at the wedding in Cana, for soon you will be getting married."

I wrote Danny in Chicago about Edie's decision. Mom thought that Edie ought to do it and I did too but Danny wasn't Catholic and Sis', in the middle of all she was going through, was afraid that Danny would want to come to see her and talk—and worse, try to talk her out of it. I knew that my sister wasn't chicken; she'd proved that since we were kids, going out for cross country, always having a job of some kind and, most especially, going off to war.

That night in the living room I thought I could see changes in my sister. It's hard to describe but it was as if I could see the Holy Spirit at work in her already, beginning to define her spiritual formation. Mom said she noticed it too and because of that we decided that one of us must write to Danny. I said let's draw straws but Mom said that she and Danny had become very close while he lived with us but that the three of us—Edie, Danny, and I—were, as she put it, generational, and that might make it easier for Danny to accept and deal with from either Edie or me. The task became mine.

After her exploratory travels Edie had decided to apply to the Sisters of Mercy, whose main missions were nursing and teaching. They were founded in Dublin, Ireland, by Catherine McAuley, Edie said and that background coupled with ours drew her also. The choir sisters are charged with charities outside the convent and the lay sisters with matters of the convent. Edie asked to be a choir sister and her extensive nursing experience, she said, seemed attractive to them. The first house of this order in America was established in Pittsburgh in 1843. Edie said she hoped for an assignment there because of its history and because Pittsburgh was not too far from Cossins. When Mom questioned her about that Edie acknowledged that final vows would lie about five years down the road but once professed she hoped to be able to come home once in awhile.

In addition to explaining all of this to Danny in my letter I knew he'd be interested in the requirements for acceptance which are quite simple and straightforward.

In general, I wrote to Danny, these are the basic requirements:

- You must be a Catholic woman.
- You must be single, since you will be married to God.
- You must not have any dependent children, or no children at all.
- You must not have any debts.
- You must be healthy.
- You must be 18 to 40 years old, although there are exceptions to this.

I didn't hear back from Danny right away but after about a week I got a phone call. It was good to hear his voice again. He was in love with my sister so I knew that all of this must be very difficult for him, but Danny and I had become close friends, especially when he lived with us. I wasn't expecting his question but after we hung up and I had time to sit by the phone and think, his question was not only logical but necessary.

"Hi, Liz," he said.

"Hi, Danny, how's Chicago? How's Loyola?" I wanted to picture his parents' apartment, wanted to see him sitting or standing with the phone but couldn't. Edie had said he had sent her pictures but she didn't show them to me and I felt that asking could be intrusive, especially since during her travels she'd seemed withdrawn.

"I got the stuff about Edie and the Sisters of Mercy," he said.

I waited for him to continue but he didn't. "What did you think?" I said. "How did it make you feel?"

After a long pause he said, "To be honest, Liz," he said, "I felt sick to my stomach. And I wondered how Mom took it." Danny had taken to calling our parents "Mom" and "Dad" while he was living with us and they liked it.

"Of course," I said, "Dad isn't here but Mom was more than supportive."

"I was afraid of that," Danny said. "You know, Liz, that after the navy I had two dreams. One was to find and marry Edie. The other was law school."

I thought he might continue, actually hoped that he would, but again all I could hear was his breathing on the other end. I knew this was going to be hard but it was turning out worse than I expected. I felt myself squirming, wishing it was Edie's call and not mine. I took a deep breath. "I don't know what to say, Danny. When Edie told us Mom and I were very happy for her and I know Dad would have been too. People say things about our loved ones looking down from heaven and smiling on us when something beautiful happens to us. I don't believe that. But I do believe that if he were here he'd be thrilled."

"Thrilled?" Danny said, almost in disbelief. "Locked away? No grandchildren? No husband to love? What's to be thrilled?"

"I know it's hard to understand, Danny. It has a lot to do with our Catholic faith. Once a priest was asked what good these brothers and sisters do behind the walls of monasteries and convents. He said that they are like batteries for the engines of the rest of us. Batteries are silent and for the most part invisible, behind, so to speak, the walls of the car surrounding them. But they are silent energy waiting to be called on. Brothers and sisters in convents and monasteries are a kind of constant energy for the rest of us in their incessant prayers."

"Forgive me, Liz, but I don't get it. What I do get is that my heart is broken, my love lost, my dream shattered."

I waited. I could hear Danny choke up. A tear ran down my cheek and into my mouth and I licked its salt from my lip. I wanted to hold Danny in my arms and let him cry on my shoulder. My heart was breaking now too for both Danny and my sister, even after my happiness before at the news of her new journey. God, I thought, this is like the guy who survives the beach at Normandy to come home and die under the wheels of a bus.

"Are you still there? Danny?" I said.

"Yes, I'm still here. I'm still in Chicago. But that's about all."

"Will you still come to see us, Danny? Please come to see us, Danny. Mom and I still love you. And Edie still loves you. I know it's hard, Danny, but try to be happy for her. She's a good girl, Danny, and I know right now that you can't believe it but she loves you more now than ever."

It had been three years since that phone call from Danny. And he had come to visit just a few times. Mom insisted he stay with us when he did come. He had Edie's room and when he came down for breakfast I thought I could see still the pain in his eyes. The three of us did things together, picnics, movies, church. Danny had never been to a Mass before and I was a bit surprised to see more than a flicker of interest on his part.

Mom and Dr. Estes had seen each other from time to time over the years outside of the clinical situation. His first name was Carroll. His friends called him Cary and we did, too. Unlike Dad and the famous movie star Cary was of medium height but also with a trim build. I looked for some connection between Mom and her doctor but couldn't find one until one evening after a sad movie in which the female lead lost her husband, a pilot, in a raid on a Japanese island in the South Pacific. I stopped to use the ladies' room on the way out. Mom and Cary waited for me on a bench in the lobby and when I approached them I noticed they were holding hands. Oddly, perhaps, I wasn't surprised. Mom said she had talked to our priest about some things and he told her to move forward, carefully. I had no problem with that. Dad had been gone for three years and Mom did everything carefully.

Danny finished up at Loyola. His parents, of course, had known all about Edie so they hoped he'd stay there and find a law firm. Danny told them it was time for him to move on and that he'd been it touch with a two-man firm in Cossins that was looking to expand. He also told them that he'd developed a soft spot in his heart for Cossins and small town life. His dad reminded him that there was more money to be made in Chicago and Danny agreed but said that his heart was more important then his bank account. Of course his mom asked him if he could handle Edie's ghost. He told her that he needed to face that and that if he couldn't get past it he'd have to find a way to deal with it. She asked him about all his friends in Chicago. He told her that the war had somehow driven a wedge there and that he'd made a lot of new friends in Cossins. They loved him so, of course, they let him go. There were no brothers or sisters so they kissed him into his car, told him his room was always ready and reminded him to get an apartment with a guest room.

❖❖❖ ❖❖❖ ❖❖❖

It happened, of all places, on the trip to Chateau-Thierry. I guess enough time had passed and one day at dinner Mom said, "Why don't we all go down to the lake for a few days?"

The original plan was for the four of us—Mom and Cary and Danny and I—to go down in Cary's car. I sensed still some reservation on Mom's part to going down in separate cars and creating the impression that we were two couples in the closest sense. But Cary said that he needed to be free to respond to a call from the hospital so that it would be better to take two cars. Mom called Mr. Branam at the Edgewater Beach Cottages to reserve our cabin and she and Cary left first. After Danny and I picked up some supplies we left in Danny's car. Mom didn't say anything but it was perfectly clear in that unspoken manner that women, especially mothers, have that Cary and Danny would share one of the bedrooms and Mom and I would take the other one. Of course I couldn't read the guy's minds but I had to give them credit for saying nothing. I didn't know how free of Edie Danny had become until, as the lovely Missouri countryside swept past us, the wind blowing our hair, Danny turned down the volume on the car radio sending Helen O'Connell and "Green Eyes" off into a cornfield.

"Remember that phone call?" he said. "The one we had about the requirements to become a nun?" I nodded and said yes. I didn't know what was coming but I sensed that there was still not enough daylight between Danny and my sister.

"There are two questions that I failed to ask you, Liz. If it's okay, I'd like to ask them now." I wasn't sure what they were but suddenly I wished that we were all together in Cary's car. On the other hand Danny had become almost like a brother to me. I'd never dreamed of having a brother but it was nice, especially since Edie was away to have, so to speak, another family figure around.

"Sure, Danny," I said, "go ahead."

"One is kinda personal and the other more professional. Let me take the personal one first. When you recited the requirements to me I was hoping you'd say that one of them was, this isn't easy, Liz—that one of them was virginity."

Of course, I knew that Edie and Danny had been together. She'd told me about that night of Waikiki Beach and the weekend in the hotel so it would be unfair of me to call it shock but coming from Danny the question touched a nerve in me. It would be some time later before I realized what had happened. "As you say, Danny, that's about as personal as it gets and I prefer not to go into any detail—actually, I don't have any detail—but to answer you directly virginity is not one of the requirements." I waited but Danny didn't say anything. He sighed softly but I couldn't tell if it was in resignation or relief. I waited for the second question. It was clear that he was still deeply in love with Edie.

"The second question," he said, "is about health, that the postulant must be in good health. We know that Edie has a bona fide phobia, an unreasonable fear of men and I wondered if . . ."

"Of course, Danny, you wondered if that condition might disqualify Edie as a postulant. I don't know and Edie has said nothing to me about it and I don't know if she's said anything to Mom." Danny was steering with his left hand, his right lay on the seat beside him. I reached over and put my left hand on his right.

"Danny, I don't know what to say except that it might be better not to bring all this up when we get to Chateau-Thierry."

We didn't own it. They don't sell the cabins at the lake. But over all those years Chateau-Thierry had become our second home and when Mom or Dad called Mr. Branam to reserve it there had, as far as I knew, never been a problem. I think he did that for a lot of folks who had left part of their lives in the walls of their favorite cabin.

Mom and Cary were already there when Danny and I walked in. Something hit me. It was the first time I'd been there since Dad had been taken from us. I can't say it was an odor like his shaving lotion or the smell of his freshly washed jeans. It must have been, as I said, in the walls. Whatever, Dad was there and I thought, also, that I could sense, if not smell, my sister's presence. A small tear trapped itself in the corner of my right eye. So they were here, both of them and I wondered if I came back in five or even ten years if they would be here still. The day would come, I knew, when Mom might be too old to come back here and Edie too much in love with our Lord even to think about Chateau-Thierry. Dad would never come back of course but what about me? Would I, one day bring my children here? Could I bring my children here?

Danny and I hugged Mom and Cary and we all went outside to the Adirondack chairs and the first drink of the long weekend. The dogwood trees and the bluebirds were anticipating spring. The evening sun was warm through my sweater but the lake water was too cool for a dip. I smiled to myself as I saw my sister lose her top in that dive off the platform, especially in contrast to the habit she was wearing now. I'm sure nostalgia, like mosquitoes, has a place in our lives but they both hurt. Cary was on one end of the semi-circle, Danny at the other with Mom and me in the middle. Cary's chair was closer to Mom's than was Danny's to mine and when Mom put her glass down each time he placed his hand gently on hers. I wanted so to put Dad in Cary's chair but my powers of levitation, of recreation, simply were not there.

As the light faded gradually across the lake we moved inside to the round kitchen table in the middle of the room. Mom and Cary had their backs to the kitchen and Danny and I faced them. I poured a second drink all around and Mom stuck a noodle casserole in the oven. Even though no one was smoking I cracked two windows slightly on either side of the room and the scent of pine trees stole into the room to mix with the sizzling cheese on the casserole as it sat on the open door of the oven. As seemed always the case at Chateau-Thierry peace descended like a gentle fog, wrapping us in incomplete family.

Danny and I cleaned up the dishes and put the cooled casserole in the fridge. Mom had lighted a cigarette. Cary asked me for a little more wine for him and Mom. Two small candles in the middle of the table provided the only light. Danny and I sat down. Danny said he wished Edie were here. Thinking probably that there was nothing he could say under the circumstances, Cary took Mom's left hand in his, slid a diamond ring on her finger and said, "Marie, will you marry me?" There was a pause. Mom looked at the ring, then at me and then, arms around Cary's neck, said, "I will."

There are those times in life like divorce and death and serious accident when it is almost impossible to know what to say. Then there are happy times, even glorious times like the priesthood and the sisterhood and moving a long way from home that also leave one speechless, either literally or emotionally. This was one of those times. Cary's proposal and Mom's immediate acceptance had thrown us all into a dilemma of silence. It wasn't that we weren't happy, including Mom and Cary, for them. It was like Christmas as a child after all the presents have been opened and it's time to clean up the room and take a second look at the loot: What's next? Where do we go from here? Is it really the end of it or is it the beginning of the year that leads to the next Christmas? I knew that some one should, must say something.

I went around the table to Mom. I hugged her. "Mom," I said, "I'm so happy for you." Then, remembering Danny, "We're so happy for you and Cary." I kissed her on the cheek and hugged Cary.

Then, again, Danny said, "I wish Edie were here. Have you told her?"

"Of course," Mom said, "I didn't know, didn't even suspect. We could call her now but there is no phone. There is a Western Union in town. Maybe . . ."

I didn't want this joy to turn into confusion. "When we get home I need to go to Pittsburgh. I could see her if it's permissible." I turned to Danny. "If you have the time, maybe you could go with me. I know she'd like to see you."

"Pittsburgh?" Cary said.

"Yes, I told Mom. I have two novels I've been working on for some time. One is a war story, World War Two, that needs a major revision. The other is a novel based on the life of Marjorie Kinnan Rawlings that's almost ready. I've been searching for a publisher and it was Edie, actually, who mentioned one in Pittsburgh called Dorrance Publishing. Been in business for around forty years. Dad would have called it an old line firm. He said it's always better to deal with old line firms. They want to see me. Said to bring the Rawlings manuscript. I could check with Edie and if it's okay we could see her and tell her the news in person. How does that sound, Mom?"

She looked at Cary, took his hand then studied her new ring. "I would like that," she said. "In person is always better don't you think, Hon'?"

It had been years. I'd never heard her call anyone "Hon'" except Dad. She always called Edie and me "Dear" or "Sweetie."

"Yes. If it were I," Cary said, "I'd prefer a visit from Liz' and Danny. And you and I can talk to your priest about a date and procedures."

Mom blushed. I didn't need to but remembering Saint Catherine reminded me that that, yes, my mom was every bit a woman still. I turned to Danny. "What about you," I said. "Ever been to Pittsburgh?"

I wrote to Edie. I wasn't sure if phone calls were acceptable while she was a postulant and, although she had given me a list of the rules, I had misplaced it. She said that she could see me briefly but not Danny and wanted to know if the big news I'd mentioned was good or bad. Danny said no, that under the circumstances he preferred not to go and besides, as a new member of the firm, he needed to get to work. The lady I'd spoken to at Dorrance, a Mrs. Ashley, said that if they accepted my manuscript she'd be my project manager. She said also that as I was coming alone she'd be happy to arrange for a room nearby.

I saw Edie in an anteroom at the convent, just the two of us. She wore what I suppose you would call a habit of sorts. It was not the kind of habit I was accustomed to seeing on the streets but then she was not yet a nun. We hugged and cheek-kissed. She looked happy and perhaps a bit rosier and fuller of cheek. We caught up on what was going on at home and then she said as if not able to wait any longer, "Is everything alright?"

We sat in two wooden chairs facing each other. I took her hands in mine. "We were at the lake, Mom and Cary and Danny and I. After dinner and the dishes we settled in for a last sip of wine. There was a lull and suddenly Cary slid a ring on Mom's finger and asked her to marry him. She looked genuinely surprised and of course so were Danny and I. I didn't know what was coming but almost without a moment's hesitation Mom said yes.

Edie sat still and quiet for awhile. She smiled and looked at her hands, especially her left hand.

"Are you okay?" I asked. "Are you sure you're doing the right thing?" I took her left hand in mine.

"Is anyone ever sure that they're doing the right thing?" she said. "Anyway, I've got time, lots of time, to find out."

"Yes," I said. "We're happy for you, Sis, but we miss you."

She withdrew her left hand from mine. She looked up at me. "You and Danny?" she said. "I didn't know."

"No, Edie, please," I said. "It's nothing like that. The four of us had finished dinner. Danny has his own place but Mom makes it clear he's always welcome. Sort of out-of-the-blue Mom says why don't we all go down to the lake for a few days. Of course Cary and Danny shared our room and Mom and I the other one. We talked of you and the fun we'd had in the past when Dad was alive. I didn't say anything of course but had to smile when I remembered the time you lost your top. You're very loved, you know. I asked Danny if he wanted to come here with me, but the fact that he couldn't see you and is still in love with you ruled it out. Besides he said he needed to get to work at his new job. I hope it's not as hard for you, Sis', as it is for him."

"You know, Liz," she said, "I can't answer that. But I can say that I'll never forget him."

Sisterhood, I thought. How many different kinds there were. Here we sit, a sisterhood within a sisterhood. "We can't recreate the past can we, Edie?"

"What do you mean?"

"Two girls, two sisters on the bed growing up; two girls at the lake playing in the water; two girls at Mass, how you took my hand as I approached the Holy Eucharist for the first time. And now after school, after sharing what clothes would fit, after the war, after college, here we sit, again together but facing life from two such different vantage points.

"Danny can't understand the idea that you don't love him any more."

Edie looked at me more directly than I'd ever seen her do before. She smiled. A tiny bell tinkled somewhere. She stood up and I stood up. We hugged. "Don't hurt him," she said, "just tell him there's a greater love." I stood, tears on my face, and watched Edie, my sister, walk away, back to the Lord. It would be a long time before I saw her again, I knew, and I hadn't even told her about my book.

ELEVEN

CROSS CREEK, FLORIDA, MIGHT BE called a hamlet. It's not big enough to be called a village and certainly not enough to be called a town. But it's where Marjorie Kinnan Rawlings lived and where she and her husband bought a large spread when Marjorie was an aspiring writer in New York City. They moved to Cross Creek but, not long after, her husband grew tired of the isolation and a country style of life so foreign to a New Yorker. With regret he left to return to New York and Marjorie became close friends with a local, young colored woman who figured in many of Rawlings' writings.

Marjorie began by writing short stories set in New York. She sent these to her friend and editor, Max Perkins at Charles Scribner's and Sons Publishing House. Perkins had developed a reputation for discovering and aiding new writing talent including Ernest Hemingway and F. Scott Fitzgerald.

In letters to Perkins Marjorie talked of life at Cross Creek. Perkins decided to visit Cross Creek to see what was going on with his friend. On the porch one night at Marjorie's clapboard cottage in Cross Creek, so the story goes, over a glass or two of whiskey, Perkins advised Rawlings to forget about New York as subject matter and concentrate instead on the place that it was clear to him had invaded and captured her heart.

She took Perkins's advice and the results were several books including the autobiographical *Cross Creek* and the novel, *The Yearling*. Probably the most offered advice to young writer is to write about what you know. Obviously, Marjorie knew a lot about New York but maybe her heart was not in it and because of that and because of personal reasons we may never know she found her Shangrila amid the swamps and orange groves of Central Florida.

I wrote to Mrs. Rawlings and told her a little about myself. I told her I needed two things, some authenticity for my book and her permission to finish it and get it published. I mentioned Dorrance, my publisher who had seen the unfinished manuscript and had suggested this letter and a possible visit to Cross Creek. I suggested a date and asked also if I could bring a friend. She wrote back and said that she could give us lunch and the better part of the day and, of course, to bring the manuscript. I asked Danny after the fact and he said that he'd try to get some time off. His boss was a guy with a manuscript in the proverbial bottom drawer of his desk so he said okay but no side trips to Daytona as they had a lot of work piled up. Danny offered to drive but I figured the distance at about nine hundred miles and that would mean an overnight stop somewhere so I suggested we take the train to Gainesville and catch a bus the twenty or so miles southeast to Cross Creek. Danny said he didn't see the need for all that but if that's what I wanted it was okay with him. After Edie's question about Danny and me at the convent I didn't want to muddy the waters, so to speak. After all, Edie hadn't been with the Sisters of Mercy very long and for several years she was able to leave if and when she felt her commitment was not strong enough to sustain her in her love for Jesus Christ. The train idea proved a good one. We rode coach and sat up all the way but Danny fell asleep several times and his head kept ending up on my chest.

I must say something about the train. Even though I'd seen trains coming and going through Cossins all my life this was my first train trip. In Chicago Danny had ridden the El trains and what he called a "big" train over to Michigan several times for scout camp in the summertime. The trains I saw passing through Cossins looked okay to me—after all

I had no basis for comparison. But the inside of the one Danny and I boarded for Florida was something else. Picture a train in the best old western movie you can remember. My first mistake was wearing a skirt and blouse. (I carried for a purse a shoulder bag containing a clutch bag, a change of underwear, and a fresh blouse. I would find the black, lace bra and panties a mistake also after Danny rummaged in the shoulder bag for something to eat. I was sure it wasn't his first exposure to lingerie but he blushed appropriately anyway. In addition to the shoulder bag I carried something far more valuable, the first draft of my manuscript in one of those heavy-paper fold over files with a stretch band for closing.)

I'd heard somewhere something about a thing called mohair but I had no idea what it was other than covering for a chair. The seats in the old train were covered in mohair. I don't think Danny noticed. He wore pants. Mohair on bare legs is definitely a no-no. As the trip wore on I wished that the mohair was not only the only problem but also the major one.

Danny gave me the window seat. After a few more passengers entered our car I asked Danny if he'd open the window for me. He leaned over and raised the window to a stop about halfway up. I asked him about the stop and he said the El trains in Chicago had them too to prevent folks from hanging out the window and losing their heads. I cringed. "But," I said, "There's nothing outside these windows to get caught on."

"Wait until we're under way for awhile," he said, "and I think you may get the point."

The mohair was a nuisance. It was summer so neither of us carried a sweater that I could sit on. I decided the best thing I could do was to slide the manuscript file under my legs and hope that I wouldn't get it too wet with perspiration. I had a carbon copy at home but there was something special about the original of anything. Danny asked me if he could read the manuscript on the way down. I felt uneasy saying no but then remembered what Uncle Rich had said in writing class. "I'm not a superstitious man," he said, "and you may do as you please, but people will almost certainly ask to read your work in progress and I would advise against it. That advice is older than the hills and I'm not sure where it originated but I abide by it and I advise you to also." I told Danny that and he said he understood, but I'm not sure that he did. This was my first manuscript and I thought I understood: it felt like having someone see you before you've finished dressing.

In the old westerns, you may remember, the locomotives had large, funnel-shaped stacks sticking up in the air at the front of the engine. These smokestacks were designed to throw the ash and fire sparks up into the air and, carried by the wind created by the speed of the train, away from the train. The problem was that the wind across the fields also played a part and that wind often sent smoke and sparks into the cars through the windows. When Danny had said to wait awhile and I might get the point I found out what he meant. I'd looked at Danny to say something when I felt something warm on my leg. I looked down and saw a small piece of glowing ash on my skirt. I jumped and Danny looked. Quickly, he brushed the tiny coal off my skirt and knocked it to the floor where he stepped it out with his shoe. Frightened, I threw my arms around his neck and held on. His face was only inches from mine. I could feel his breath and smell his aftershave but in his eyes I saw nothing. Or was it nothing? Or was it the soul of my sister, Edie? The hole in my skirt was about the size of a dime and through it I saw the hole in my white slip. The journey to Cross Creek was not off to a great start.

"When we get to Gainesville," Danny said, "we'll find a department store before we catch the bus to Cross Creek. After all, we don't want Mrs. Rawlings to think we're a couple of country bumpkins, do we?" As it turned out there was no fear of that. Cross Creek had left its mark on the great writer as surely as that hot coal had on my skirt.

The closest store near the train station was a pink pastel building of two storeys with the name "Belk" on the side in large script letters. I found a few replacement skirts and a white half slip to make do for the full slip with the hole in it. I asked Danny if he wanted to look for an extra shirt. I'd noticed that he hadn't brought an overnight bag. He said no, that he'd just wait for me outside the dressing room. I came out wearing a new skirt with the half-slip underneath.

"I like it," Danny said. "Plaid. And green, my favorite color. Where's the other stuff?"

I twirled around to show him the new skirt. I smiled. I took his hand. "That's an old story," I said, "and a short one. You know Mom so you might appreciate it." We sat on a bench outside the dressing room. "When Edie and I were just girls Mom taught us that whenever we bought something new in the way of clothing we should wear the new out of the store and leave the old in the changing room."

"Why?" Danny said.

"Mom had survived the Great Depression," I said. "She said that when you go shopping you probably have decent, clean clothes on. After you leave the store in your new stuff if you leave the old stuff behind it should send a message to the clerk that you're thinking of someone in need who could use it. She told us to think of it as a kind of private, personal Good Will."

This time Danny took my hand. He smiled. "Only your mom would think of that," he said. "It might work in Cossins but in Chicago they might think you're stealing the stuff." We both laughed. I paid for the skirt and slip and Danny asked the clerk where the bus station was.

The Greyhound was actually nicer than the train. Again, Danny gave me the window seat and this time I could open the window back and forth as far as I wanted to. It was to be a short ride of about twenty miles so we didn't try to nap.

"What are you reading?" I asked Danny.

"It's a flyer I picked up at the bus station."

"What's it about?"

"Mostly, the University of Florida."

"Anything interesting?"

"You learn something new every day."

"Like what?"

"Like the University of Florida was once a men's college and that it's older than the University of Chicago."

"When was it founded?"

117

"Eighteen fifty-three and Chicago was not founded until eighteen ninety."

"Who would have thought? I thought Florida was just a swamp when Chicago started building skyscrapers."

"Me, too," Danny said.

"Hmm," I said, "that's interesting. My little Drury College was founded in eighteen seventy-three so it's older than Chicago, too." I poked Danny with my elbow. "Guess you Yankees haven't got us Johnny Rebs beat in everything."

"Johnny Rebs? I thought you "show-me" guys fought on our side."

"That's a whole other story. We can do that on the way home. Looks like we're here."

We got off at the junction of U.S. 301 and a country road with a sign that said "Cross Creek." An arrow pointed down the road but there was no indication of how far down the road. We then noticed a wooden wagon. Standing next to it was an old Negro man smoking a cigarette. "Mornin'," he said, and touched the brim of his cap.

"Mrs. Rawlings?" Danny said.

"Yessir," the old man said. "She sent me. Name's Carl. Carl King." He took a drag on his cigarette, tossed it onto the dirt road and crushed it with his field shoe.

Danny held out his hand. "Name's Danny Landy." Carl looked at Danny's hand but didn't take it.

"Guess we better get down the road," Carl King said. He climbed up on the short front seat and motioned us to a double in back.

Danny helped me up. "Ladie's name is Miss Endsley," Danny said. Carl turned around and touched his cap again. "Far to go?" Danny said.

"Maybe a mile," Carl said, "maybe two."

On the left side of the road for at least a mile were nothing but orange groves and the scent was wonderful if a bit cloying. On the right an unending stand of large pine trees so tall and close together that, even on this early summer morning, no light could be seen inside the forest. The sun shone bright on the road but the trees on either side kept us cool from a soft breeze that crossed us as from a huge electric fan. Except for the crosswind the only sound came from the hoofs of the black mare as they padded over the well-worn dirt. At first I didn't but now I understood Carl's long-sleeved flannel shirt: It wasn't hot on the road and the sweat that might come later would be absorbed by the fabric. Most writers enjoy solitude and I saw why Mrs. Rawlings might have chosen Cross Creek.

The mare came to a stop by herself in front of a small clapboard house. I'd heard nothing from Carl nor from the snap of a rein. So this must be it, the home of Marjorie Kinnan Rawlings, New York girl turned Florida Cracker.

Danny and I left the wagon and stood in the road in front of the house. Carl waited until we were clear and moved off slowly toward the back of the house and a lean-to type shed. On the front porch was a substantial looking wooden table. On top of the table was a black, standard typewriter like mine. I couldn't tell the make of the machine but my writer's heart responded like a child who'd seen a familiar friend.

Strangely, perhaps, I had never seen a picture of Marjorie Kinnan as a young woman nor of Mrs. Rawlings the famous writer. When it seemed either that there was no one at home or that the lady had forgotten our date, she appeared in the doorway of the porch. Of course, from my research I knew that she had been here for many years and of her early time in New York. I don't know what I had expected, perhaps like the American in Europe who is so easily recognized by his shoes, or perhaps a woman in a dress with a line down the center with a skyscraper painted on one side and an orange tree on the other. I had to remind myself that I had not written a biography of the great writer but a work of fiction. The manuscript I held in my hand portrayed a woman who looked almost nothing like the one standing on the porch with a cigarette in one hand and a heavy, ceramic coffee cup in the other. She studied us but did not smile.

"Well," she said, "don't just stand there. I understand you're from Missouri so get up here and show me what you got."

I looked at Danny. He took my hand and we climbed the four steps to the porch. She shook our hands and motioned to a couple of chairs on the other side of the door, away from her writing table. We sat down.

"Didn't know you were married," she said. "For some reason I thought the friend you mentioned was a female. Besides Carl, my only friend is a woman. Good to see another man once in awhile. Want some coffee? Want something in it?"

A beautiful, young, Negro woman appeared in the doorway. Marjorie pulled her writing chair from behind the table and sat facing us. Danny sat, legs crossed horizontally as most men do. I sat both feet on the floor, my manuscript folder in my lap. Mrs. Rawlings looked, spoke, and acted as if she had lived in this cabin all her life.

"Sissy," she said, "please get two coffees for our guests. Save the bottle for later."

The subject of my book didn't ask again if we wanted anything in our coffee and I didn't ask, although I preferred milk and sugar. I knew Danny drank his black and I knew, also, that before we left we would drink a whiskey with a lady from New York who might not have had too much of a taste for the stuff before she found Cross Creek. She thanked Sissy for the coffee and invited her to sit but Sissy said she had to attend to lunch.

"Danny and I are just friends," I said.

She said, "I didn't see a car. Must have come by bus."

"Actually, train and bus," I said. I thought I knew where she was going with this but I didn't mention Edie. I thought that might get too complicated.

"Engaged?" she said, looking at my hand.

"No," I said, "Danny's our family attorney. He's never been to Florida."

"There's only two parts to Florida," she said, "the sand that's growin' tourists and the sand that's growing taters and oranges. Right now you're in the latter." She looked at Danny. "And young man" she said, "you don't need to bother looking for bathing suits around these parts." She called the girl. "Sissy," she said, "show these folks around the estate, will you, while I look at a manuscript. After lunch and a glass of Bourbon I'll be out of the mood."

I handed my manuscript to Mrs. Rawlings feeling privileged but also a bit nervous as I suppose a young mother might in handing her child over to a stranger. She took it as though she had done so hundreds of times, the gesture causing me to feel less privileged than I had moments ago. My studies had lead me to believe that most writers of some prominence seldom if ever deigned to read the work of neophytes, that thought slightly restoring my confidence. We left her sitting behind her typewriter with a fresh cigarette, new coffee and my child.

Sissy wore a print shift over her slim frame, her hair natural in a kerchief. It was obvious that she didn't wear a bra, maybe didn't own one, and also that she didn't need one. Her feet were bare as she showed us around and pointed out a small stable and a few sheds and outbuildings. She seemed most interested and somewhat proud of the orange groves which she helped to care for and which seemed to give her a sense of propriety. In her I sensed sensitivity and culture that could not have come from Cross Creek. I wondered if she painted or had taken up writing, so to speak, at the feet of Marjorie Rawlings. I wanted to ask her questions about her childhood and education but it seemed somehow inappropriate at the moment. Danny said later that he'd wanted to ask Sissy if Mrs. Rawlings had competent legal counsel regarding the property and the sale of the oranges and other crops but that he knew that would be taken as prying especially in the outback anywhere and he guessed especially in the outback of Marjorie Kinnan Rawlings. I'd always loved horses and I asked Sissy if the black mare that picked us up was the only horse on the property. She said that a man down the road who helped with the smudge pots during freezes had a couple of riding horses and that she and Missy, meaning Mrs. Rawlings I assumed, borrowed them for a ride now and then, to clear their heads she said.

Danny asked if there was a creek at Cross Creek. Sissy said yes, but it had pretty much dried up over the years.

"Do you want to see it?" she asked.

"No, that's okay," Danny said. "Thanks anyway."

Sissy picked three oranges for us and offered her penknife for peeling. At first I didn't see where the knife came from—it couldn't have come from her bra—and then I saw a small pocket in the side of her dress. Sissy seemed content enough but I sensed a curiosity—not a restlessness but a curiosity—about what life might hold for her beyond Cross Creek, that there might be more than orange groves waiting out there for her somewhere.

I saw Danny check his watch. So did Sissy so we headed back to the house. I was anxious to hear what Marjorie had to say about my work and if she would give me permission to publish it. Also, I was hungry.

As we walked toward the house I smiled. Marjorie had referred to Danny as "young man" and I knew he must be around forty. I was in my thirties, not far behind, so I wondered if I were a "young woman." I guessed the writer to be in her sixties but it was hard to tell as the rugged life in this outback, the sun and the sweat and the constant battles with nature and finances, revealed itself in lines on the face and on the soul.

The lady sat where we had left her behind her typewriter. My manuscript was back in its folder and next to her hand and coffee cup. She pointed to the chairs and we sat down. Sissy went straight to the kitchen, I guessed to finish preparing our meal. I had become interested in the social structures of the area and wondered if Sissy would be eating with us.

"Young woman," she said, "you obviously have more than ordinary talent and I encourage you to pursue your work. As far as the manuscript goes I've met with a couple of my biographers and you have equaled or surpassed them in capturing me on paper in fiction, something I would not know how to do myself. As it *is* fictional and biographical at the same time I would not know how to correct you even if you needed it, and you don't. I don't agree with all the segments of your portrayal but then it's fiction and you are certainly entitled to poetic license."

"Do I . . . ?" I began.

"I'm not sure you need it," she said, "but, yes, you have my permission to publish. Now, while Sissy finishes up with lunch let's relax with a drink."

She produced, apparently from a shelf under her desk, three lowball glasses and a wine glass. Into the lowball glasses she poured whiskey from a square bottle, about three fingers in each. As if at a signal, Sissy came and Marjorie handed her the empty wine glass and she returned to the kitchen. The writer raised her glass in a toast and we followed. "I have whitelightnin' if you prefer it," she said. Danny and I smiled, sipped the whiskey, and said nothing. I'd have preferred sharing some wine with Sissy but I'd tasted liquor before and, as an aperitif, it's supposed to help mask the hunger.

Without at all feeling supercilious I expected cornpone and catfish for lunch, which would have been just fine with me. After all, Cossins, Missouri, is not exactly uptown, either. Instead we had chicken fried steak on rice with black-eyes peas on the side. For dessert there was cornbread and jam with buttermilk. I've loved buttermilk since I was a little girl but I could tell that Danny was doing his duty by drinking his. After dinner there was black coffee with a shot in it. Oh, and there were four of us—Sissy joined us at the table, with her wine glass, now full.

It was time to go. The bus would be at the junction within half an hour. We stood in the front yard with appreciations and thank you's. I had my manuscript in hand. I looked into Sissy's eyes and saw there a sisterhood. I didn't know what was acceptable but I went to her for a hug and kissed her on the cheek. Somehow, I knew without thinking that this would not do for Marjorie so we shook hands. It occurred to me later that among the four of us Marjorie needed and wanted a hug and maybe even a kiss more than any of us. Danny shook hands with the two women and suddenly as if from nowhere Carl appeared with the wagon and the black mare. I am more sentimental than emotional so I had to pull away in that pain we all know from the knowledge that I would never see this woman, Marjorie Kinnan Rawlings, again. The tears began so I turned and climbed into the wagon on Danny's hand, manuscript in the other. I waved at Marjorie and Sissy from the wagon, at these two strong, even tough, women who were used to being alone if not to loneliness and saw in their faces that they wanted us to stay. Marjorie stood in her worn corduroy pants, Sissy in her pretty shift, and I couldn't help but wonder what Marjorie looked like her first day here from New York. I would bet almost anything that, on that first day, she wore a dress but in my mind's eye I tried but couldn't picture what it looked like. My forever picture of her would print in my mind her pants and soft, flannel shirt, concealing her femininity but not her large, soft heart. I didn't really know her but I loved her.

One of the famous writers I'd studied in college said that writers, especially fiction writers, have room in their lives for only one love beyond their writing. I wondered if Marjorie missed her husband and then I wondered where beautiful Sissy's man was. And then I looked at Danny.

The ride back to the junction was a carbon copy of the first one. Carl King was again a man not of few words but of no words. He was a hard read, as they say. My writer's mind could not resist trying to find him inside his lovely, brown garment of skin. Was he, I thought, a prisoner of the past, a case of arrested development stopped in his tracks by the sin of slavery suffered by his forebears? Did he, I wondered, talk to his family, if he had one, to his neighbors, or was his taciturnity a self-imposed, silent protest against what he saw as a trap he'd stepped into and could not free himself from. I did right then what I'd done all my life, thanks to the Lord and to my mom, I prayed for Carl King, nothing special, just as one child of God for another. I knew, as I had with Marjorie, that I'd never see Carl King again, but I knew also that Carl and I, like Sissy and I, were really fellow travelers bound for the same place on different roads.

The bus was on time and this time I gave Danny the window seat, as I would in Gainesville on the train, not wanting, of course for him to get burned, especially not on his lap, but because the inside seat was more easily accessible to the rest room and I knew that it would soon be time for the lemonade and the whiskey to start to work.

As we boarded the train in Gainesville I became aware that I needed a shower, a shampoo, and fresh clothes. I'd changed to the underwear and blouse I carried in my bag but there was no way to wash up and I'd brought no deodorant so I had to trust to what I hoped was Danny's male obliviousness to such feminine concerns.

We were but shortly out of Gainesville when I felt Danny's head on my shoulder and heard the soft breath of sleep. His head rested on my right shoulder, his face but inches from my breast. I could smell his hair and whatever he wore on it and his skin through the perspiration of the trip and of the Cross Creek adventure. My boyfriend in college, David Foster, and I had danced together and hugged goodnight at my front door and I knew that the sexes carried different scents but Danny's was different from David's and different even from my father's. I knew, also, that animals were attracted to each other by scent and, although I was aware that we were animals or, at best, mammals, the thought that I could be attracted to a man through the sense of scent was not only completely foreign to me but also disconcerting, if not embarrassing. Could I, I thought, at thirty-six be discovering for the first time something so basic, so elemental, so, actually, sexy? And a second question, coming perhaps from inexperience: Is this what it's like? Is this what falling in love is like? I began to feel uneasy but, except to go to the rest room, I couldn't move, couldn't disturb Danny's sleep. I felt things I'd never felt before, female things, feminine things, connection things between us like invisible threads pulling us together. I wanted to hold Danny. Actually, I wanted to kiss him, to do more than kiss him, the thought of which was in itself a thread that pulled me, or tried to pull me away from him.

And then it came to me, didn't wash over me but punched me in the chest: I was falling in love with Edie's man, with my own sister's man. And I couldn't get away, not even to go to the bathroom.

I knew from life and from my writing that life was not simple but surely it could not be this complicated. Just as the moisture started Danny woke up. "Where are we?" he said, rubbing his eyes and sitting up straight. I dabbed my eyes with a tissue. While he looked out the window I studied his face from the side, at the sleep in his eyes and at the stubble on his chin. "I wish I knew," I said. "I wish I knew."

TWELVE

Mom and Cary were married in the side chapel of our church, St. Ambrose. Preparations were minimal. Mom was a widow and Cary had never been married before. It was simple and beautiful. Mom wore a knee length, off-white dress and carried her white Bible which, after all these years, was more the color of Mom's dress than its original white. Cary wore a navy blue suit, white shirt, and solid maroon tie. Of course, Danny and I were there and Uncle Rich came with his girlfriend, Blanche, which, although no one said anything, I know must have made Mom happy in the wake of the old gossip about Uncle's girlfriend's being a Bradley rather than a Blanche.

Praise God, Edie was given, as she put it, a dispensation to attend. Since we know that God is in charge of everything I have to believe that his hand was in on the dispensation despite the fact that Edie, even though a postulant in a convent, could not have been immune to the electricity I felt between Danny and me as we stood in the front pew, Danny between us sisters.

The service was short but beautiful. Uncle Rich gave his sister away and the tears I shed were for Dad's absence, although, man and gentleman that he was, I suspect he would have wanted it this way. Everyone likes to talk about weddings and funerals spawning either new romances or closer family ties so I couldn't imagine what might be going through the minds of Danny and Edie and Uncle Rich. I was afraid even to think of what might be going through mine if I allowed anything at all, especially with Danny standing next to me and my sister on his other side. I was also a bit ashamed of myself. Instead of really paying attention to the service I found myself trying to picture the complexities of this situation unrolling in a movie.

The reception at the house was nice. Blanche and I did the simple decorations and Uncle Rich and Danny provided the refreshments, all from the local deli and the liquor store.

Mom and Cary started their honeymoon at the Chase Hotel in St. Louis but wouldn't say where else they were going. Uncle Rich and Danny took the twin beds in the guest room and Edie and I took our beds in our room. Blanche was honored with Mom's room. I remembered as we each crawled under the covers that Edie had said as she was getting ready to leave for the convent that we would never lie together on one of the beds again and talk as we had since childhood. Oh, how I wanted to do that again just once more before she went back for her work toward final vows. I didn't know what sisters—that is, Catholic Sisters—wore to bed but Edie went straight to her dresser, pulled out a pair of pajamas, put them on and crawled into her bed.

I waited for maybe five minutes, afraid that she might say something or stop me, and then I slipped out of my bed and into hers and took her hand. She took mine and we lay there in silence I hoped thinking about the past, about all that we meant to each other all those years. But this time we were unable to talk. The biggest personal thing on my mind was Danny and I certainly couldn't talk about him there, next to my sister, the woman Danny wanted to marry, the man who was just yards away in the same house. And I don't know if Edie wanted or was even permitted to talk about the biggest thing in her life, the convent. So we just lay there together, sisters, as we had a hundred times before as girls, holding hands in silence until we fell asleep.

A couple of months later I was busy putting finishing touches on book one, the Rawlings story, and preparing more notes on book two, the Pacific Theater novel of World War II, when I heard a knock on the door of my writing room.

"Come in," I said. I had no idea who it was but I was dressed so, unless it was Jack the Ripper, it didn't matter.

"Are you busy?" Danny said. "Don't want to bother you."

"I'm very busy," I said, "but you couldn't bother me negatively under any circumstances. Have a seat." Danny grinned at my remark and I thought I saw the start of a blush. He kissed me on the forehead and sat down on the bed.

"Have you ever been to Chicago?" Danny said.

"No," I said, "but I've heard about the Cubs and the Museum of Art and Al Capone."

Danny laughed. "That's what they all say. Actually, they call it "The City Beautiful." It's fall and the leaves in the parks should be just right by now. I've got to go up to Loyola on a matter related to my new job. My boss said he'd like to get away himself but can't take the time. I thought if you've got Marjorie ready to send to Pittsburgh, your publishers, Dorrance, isn't it?"

"What is it, Danny?"

"I hoped maybe you could go with me. I'd like you to meet my parents. I could show you the sights. Oh, and there's a spare bedroom off the kitchen."

At that moment he looked like a young boy asking his girl to go to the prom. "Actually," I said, "this manuscript is ready. I'd thought of delivering it in person but they said I could mail it, that I'd been up there once already. But in the interest of time I'd like to fly if that's okay with you." I didn't know how well he could read me but by this time my feelings for him ruled out a car trip or even another train, especially after the last one.

He smiled. "Your ticket is on me," he said.

I studied his shoes. He always wore the nicest shoes. "Danny," I said, "I've sold several short stories in the past and have put some money away. I never go anywhere or do much of anything so I'd really like to pay for my flight, especially since it's my first. I hope you understand." I didn't know if he would understand but after the trip to Cross Creek, in my mind, I gave him no choice. He stood between Edie and me at the wedding. I had no way of assessing the feelings of either one of them at that time, and Edie and I had not talked that night in bed, but I, standing next to him, had been plugged into an electric outlet somewhere. I couldn't risk that again and certainly not more of it.

"Of course I understand," he said, "perhaps more than you can imagine."

I didn't have a reply to that and I didn't really want one. I hoped we were not getting in over our heads, so to speak. Danny stood up. I was afraid to, afraid of a kiss or something, a kiss I wanted very much. I felt the moisture again. I was hoping for a less personal way out but it didn't come so I stood up, too, facing him. "Danny," I said, "tinkle time. I gotta go." He smiled and turned to leave. Then he turned back, took two steps toward me and, again, kissed me, this time on the cheek.

We flew out of St. Louis on a beautiful Thursday morning in October and landed not long after in Chicago. Danny's dad was working so his mother picked us up at the airport. She asked Danny if he wanted to be dropped off at Loyola on the way home but he said no, that his appointment was scheduled for the next day, Friday.

Danny wore a black suit, white shirt, and gray silk tie. He looked really sharp and professional but I couldn't help wondering if men ever got tired of wearing the same outfit every day. Someone wrote somewhere that one of the reasons women have a hard time making it to the top in business is that instead of wearing a uniform of some sort they wear costumes that look more social than serious. I don't know about that but I do know that, even if it's true, it's not likely to make a difference any time soon. Women have been wearing costumes since Cleopatra while men have been in uniform togas since Marc Antony. While it's true that even then men ran the store, so to speak, the women had more fun with cleavage and also ran the men. Oh, well, as they say, whatever. Without planning it I, too, wore a suit, black like Danny's with an unimpeded vee neck and a string of white pearls. Danny said he liked it and gave a soft whistle. I felt good, and professional, but I wouldn't want to wear it every day, even in a different color.

I'm not sure what Danny's mother knew about me or about why her son and I were running about the country together. What I did know from what Danny had told me was that, when she looked at me she must have expected to see the girl in the picture Danny had brought home in his wallet from the Pacific, the picture of my sister, Edie. I also knew that before Danny and I flew back to Cossins on Monday she'd know a lot more and she'd know it whether either Danny or I wanted her to know it. When it comes to women, especially mothers, you can count on that.

Thursday night was one of those warm, in the sense of family, cozy, evenings. Danny's mom, Rose, was a pretty, petite woman who smiled a lot and obviously loved people and especially her husband, John, a clerk in the office of one of the Illinois Supreme Court justices in Chicago, a disjunct office. John was close to early retirement but enjoyed his work and the morning EL ride downtown with his morning paper. He was tall and rangy and reminded me of my father. He dressed like the typical downtown office worker of the time in suit and tie and, in the winter, spats. John and Rose were obviously a loving couple, actually, it appeared, still very much in love. I enjoyed watching them because they had that something that, along with my own parents, I knew I wanted for myself one day.

There were drinks before dinner in the spacious living room which offered a bay window or solarium on the street with views to the east toward Lake Michigan, the south toward downtown, and the west toward the EL tracks and the local high school. Rose said that's where they always put the Christmas tree so that the lights could be seen from the street. On the mantel was a picture of a young man in a pilot's uniform of aviator helmet and fur-lined bomber jacket. He looked like his dad, John. Rose saw me look at the picture but said nothing. The conversation was the usual background chit-chat about Chicago and family and, of course, they wanted to know about me. Apparently, they knew a lot about Edie including the fact that she had joined a religious order, but they had never met her. They asked me questions but seemed not to want to pry. I felt comfortable but, at the same time, uneasy. They knew from letters home from the war that Danny had found someone and had fallen in love and they knew that that was over but they had to find out where I, Edie's sister, fit into the picture. I felt that that was Danny's turf and was going to leave that territory to him. After all, he'd invited me, not the other way around. There was still a warmth in my belly when I looked at him sitting in the chair next to mine but, in the presence of his parents, in the home in which he'd grown up, the thrill on the train ride from Cross Creek had gone from a slow boil to a simmer. But it was still there.

There was a pause. John looked at me. "I'll bet Liz' is hungry," he said, and stood up. Without further comment we started down the long hall to the dining room. Immediately to the left was a bedroom just off the entryway to the outside stairs. On the right were two more bedrooms with a main bath between them. Then followed the large dining room and after that the kitchen. The men sat down. I followed Rose into the kitchen to see if I could help.

"This will be your room, Liz'," she said. "I'll bring your things from the hall after dinner."

She pointed to a small room just off the kitchen next to what looked like a powder room with a shower.

"In the old days," she said, "this bedroom and bath were those either of the maid or a boarder. In the latter part of the nineteenth and early part of the twentieth centuries it was not uncommon even for middle class families to employ a maid or rent a room to a boarder. Please, Liz', don't feel at all uncomfortable. We want you to have your privacy."

The room was spotless and tastefully decorated. Rose also explained that it was used for family guests and for friends from college when either of the boys came home. She didn't mention the boy in the picture on the mantel over the fireplace in the living room. As we picked up dishes from the kitchen table for dinner I wondered warmly if Danny had ever slept there. The situation was definitely awkward, given Edie and all, but it was only for a weekend—and I was close to Danny, even though not as close as I'd have liked.

We had Salisbury steak and baked potato with mixed vegetables. I hesitated, thinking it was Friday, but it wouldn't have mattered. I knew that the Landys were not Catholic. John asked me to say the blessing. I said our usual Catholic prayer and we all dug in. Danny excused himself and returned with four glasses and a bottle of cabernet. Either he didn't know or had forgotten that I prefer sweet wine. It didn't really matter. I drank it anyway. To tell the truth, nothing much mattered. I was with Danny.

Friday the men went to work, Danny to his appointment at Loyola, John to his office in the Loop.

Rose and I cleaned up after breakfast. She and John kissed before he left and I saw Rose watch her son to see if he would kiss me. He didn't. I didn't say anything because I didn't know what to say. This was only my first real day with Danny and his family and while I felt comfortable as a house guest the situation was as awkward as I had thought it might be when Danny invited me, so awkward in fact where Danny was concerned that, although I knew I was falling deeper in love with him every minute, as is so often the case when one half of a couple is on established turf and the other is not, the distance between us had increased rather than decreased. I knew the reason and it made sense but I was disturbed by the fact that I had a strong urge to get away, to get Danny back for myself alone, as if that made any sense given the constant presence of my sister, Edie, and the fact that no matter where Danny and I were we would be, our hearts would be, actually no closer at all. The whole situation was summed up for me when I had the idea, realized that I had the idea, that, oh, well, it was only for two more days. "Only for two more days" is not where you want to be when you are in the home, the family home, of the man you love. I didn't know what Rose had planned for this Friday but I hoped, at least, that it would make the time fly.

We both wore dresses and she let me borrow one of her pillbox hats and a pair of gloves. I didn't ask but I assumed that dresses, hats, and gloves were definitely de rigueur when shopping or lunching in the Loop or on Michigan Boulevard.

"You look lovely," I said, and she returned the compliment.

"Elizabeth," she said, "I'm not much for dashing about and wearing ourselves out so I have just two major stops for us today and, if you don't mind we'll leave the car at home. The EL is just a block or so away and parking is such a problem. You must go shopping at Marshall Field's. Chicagoans will tell you that if the skyscraper was born in Chicago, Field's was born in the Loop. After shopping we'll have lunch in the Oak Room. Most of the women in Chicago will tell you that such a day is not only complete but also the prelude to a romantic evening at home."

All this was as we were leaving the apartment. Rose paused for a moment as if she'd forgotten something but I knew it was the awkward remark about romance, something she knew she didn't know existed for Danny and me.

The train ride was nice. The cars had a peculiar smell but I figured that was due to interior and mechanical maintenance. I was surprised to see how close the train came to some apartment buildings; it looked like one of the residents could stick an arm out the window and touch the train as it passed. More startling were the shabby tenements we passed, tenements within but a few miles of the Loop Rose said.

Marshall Fields was the most beautiful store I'd ever seen. Of course, I hadn't traveled far—there were New York and Paris and Rome and London—but Marshall Fields had to be the Taj Mahal of department stores. There were several floors, each for a different department of wares: household, jewelry, women's clothing, men's clothing, sporting goods, children's things. It was a fairyland of goodies of all kinds, especially for a small town girl like me. Christmas was approaching. Rose bought a few gifts for friends and family. I bought a sweater for Danny and things for the family. The store was not decorated for Christmas yet but Rose mentioned the beautiful street windows that people came from miles around to see, even, she said, from nearby states like Wisconsin, Iowa, and Indiana. Marshall Fields, it appeared, was like a bright light to which the people-moths from all around were attracted. So, I thought, there are definitely advantages to life in the big city.

At the risk of sounding even more like a girl who had just fallen off a turnip truck I told Rose that the Oak Room was the most beautiful restaurant I'd ever seen. Rose accepted all this with aplomb although for someone born and bred in such a wonderful place she deserved much credit.

The Oak Room was well named. High ceilings over polished oak wall panels against which banquettes of rich leather rested, behind linen covered tables. To me it was dining from "The Arabian Nights." I don't remember what I had. It was Friday so since, as they say, old habits die hard, I'm sure I had fish. Amid the splendor of the room and the service and the wine and the ever filled water goblets, I don't remember what kind of fish and it really didn't matter.

If you know women you know that what I'm going to say next is almost as predictable as finger bowls at the Oak Room. (I had to watch Rose to know what to do with a finger bowl. If it hadn't been for the elegant ice-filled water goblets I might have sipped it.)

Of course I had no way of knowing—I couldn't read Rose's mind— what she was thinking but I could almost feel her need to mention Danny and me. The thought of it made my heart throb. Actually, I came close to bringing the subject up myself. Two women, two close women in spite of having just met, over lunch in a gilded cage, each with a heart holding the same treasure. It was the perfect setting for shared feelings. But I would wait. There was Danny. But, also, for both of us women, there was Edie, for Rose the unknown love of her older son, for me the sister I loved and respected who was now living in a Catholic convent but who had not yet taken her final vows. I would wait and, without a word or even a suggestion, so would Rose.

We left the lair of Cinderella and returned to the world of the motorman on the EL, calling out the names of the stations as they came up.

Back in the apartment after we had hung up our coats and put our purses on the beds, Rose said to me, "Come here, Liz, I want to show you something."

I followed Rose into the living room and across to the fireplace. "Liz," she said, "this is Johnny, Danny's younger brother. He looked up to Danny like probably most boys did to Babe Ruth in the thirties." Rose took the picture of Johnny down from the mantel and handed it to me. Strange the chemistry between two human beings: I could see the blood that made him and Danny brothers—he was handsome, too—but in spite of all that I felt nothing, no electricity, no magnetism, no sex appeal. As Mom used to say, "There's no accounting for taste." Walk down State Street or through Marshall Fields. Look at the couples. Ask yourself how they got together, what they saw in each other, why they fell, if they did, in love with each other.

"Not too long after Danny came home from the war, a few years I guess it was—I really don't like to think about it—Johnny decided he wanted to join the Air Force to fight in Korea as Danny had in the Pacific in the big war. He did. He got his wings at Lackland in Texas." Rose chuckled even as a tear formed in her eye.

"What is it?" I said.

"I thought it was funny at the time," Rose said.

"What?" I said.

"I don't know how many air force training facilities there are in the country," Rose said. "They were so eager for recruits that occasionally they'd honor a request for a certain base. Johnny had a girlfriend in high school. Her name was Cathy Lackland. She didn't want Johnny to go, especially after his brother's experience but Johnny was determined, as all of us Landys are, so to placate Cathy he requested Lackland Flight School and got it. Cathy cried, we all did, when Johnny left but we thought Lackland might be a good omen. It was a good name but not a good omen."

"What happened?" I said.

"Johnny was flying a mission over the Sea of Japan. We don't even know the date or if he flew alone or in formation. One day we got the notice. It was a letter from the President. They don't' come to the door for MIAs, I guess because the finality is not there yet. Night after handkerchief-twisting night we watched that big, old, black and white television as the list of MIAs scrolled across the screen, looking, praying for Johnny's name. It went on for months but nothing. We don't know to this day where Johnny is or if he's alive or dead."

By now Rose was crying and I had to join in, had to keep her company, so to speak. When I noticed my tear on the picture I handed it back to Rose. She held it to her breast and the tear dried against her dress. She put the picture back on the mantelpiece where I knew it would stay forever, even if, someday, Johnny came home.

Danny came home first, just as Rose was putting the picture of Johnny back on the mantel. He started to say something but stopped when, instantly, he summed up the situation. He looked at his mom and then at me. Rose and I were standing in front of the fireplace perhaps three feet apart. Danny came to us and took us into his arms. Rose and I went gently to them making, so to speak, a trilogy of one. There was no need to speak. Danny knew the whole story and I'd just learned it. And there was Johnny looking down at us from his station above the fireplace, looking I thought as though he wanted to comfort us, to join us, perhaps to make of our threesome a quartet. We stood there for what seemed like a long time but in reality was maybe three or four minutes in silence. The tears had stopped. The key turned in the front door lock and John came in. I don't know whether he didn't want to disturb us or if he just couldn't go through it again but he went straight to his bedroom. I heard the bathroom door close and the water running. I also smelled something like Chinese food. Rose smiled. She took my hand and Danny followed. "It's almost a family tradition," she said. "I hope you like egg foo yong." I didn't but somehow I knew there would be other choices and there were. The white wine and Saki lifted the gentle pall that had settled over us at the fireplace. We sat around the large dining room table and ate while John and Danny asked about our day. Maybe it was Johnny all the way from the Sea of Japan or just from his place on the mantel. Maybe it was the warm food on that cool October evening. Maybe it was Danny. Maybe it was because I was in love, but I felt that feeling that comes in no other way. I felt like family. But then, I wasn't thinking about Edie. I wasn't thinking about my sister and her man, the man next to me at the dining room table.

The next day, Saturday, belonged to Danny and me. He wanted to show me Chicago, his city, the place where he was born, where he went to high school, the beaches he swam and played on with his friends—and girlfriends I was sure. With Danny's looks and personality I was certain there would be girls.

Danny borrowed the family car, a 1965 tan Chrysler convertible. It was too cool to put the top down but he did it anyway. Rose lent me a gray, alpaca sweater and an orange scarf and we headed down Sheridan Road to the Outer Drive and Downtown Chicago. Danny said he'd like to start south and work our way north.

There were, first, Grant Park and Buckingham Fountain. He pointed out significant buildings like the Tribune Tower, the Merchandise Mart, and the recently completed Marina City. We took an all-too-short tour of the Art Institute and the Field Museum of Natural History; I'd told Danny of my love of nature and especially animals. There is so much to see that it's almost overwhelming especially, perhaps, for a small-town girl like me so, when Danny said he saw my eyes starting to cross he asked me if I'd ever been to a Swedish restaurant. I said no. He gave the car to what they call a valet and we entered the elegance of Kungsholm. The bustle of the city was immediately lost in the quiet serenity of the restaurant. The decor was hard to describe except to say there was a lot of white and a lot of plush and what I guessed was a very expensive menu without prices. Danny ordered for both of us and it was hot and delicious and the wine was white and sweet just, as they say, my cup of tea. The wine and Danny and the after-lunch coffee warmed me all over. How could this be, I thought. True, this was our second trip together. True, I'd spent the night in his boyhood home. True, we'd never kissed. And true, we were moving much too fast in the right and wrong direction at the same time. I may not have known exactly what I wanted but I knew I wanted Danny. I knew I wanted the first man I'd ever been in love with. And just then a tall, willowy girl passed our table apparently on her way to the restroom and, except for her blonde hair and blue eyes she could have been Edie. I looked at Danny and, thank God, he was looking at me. That was good but what happened next was not. He took my hand and kissed it. This time it was not the wine and the food that made me giddy. It was pure animal attraction. Whether you are a man or a woman reading this, but especially if you're a woman, you know what I mean—and you know what giddy does to you—and no more needs to be said. Except I love you but I could not bring myself to say it in spite of the fact that all I wanted to do was curl up in his lap and make love.

We got home around six. I was cold in spite of the fact that Danny had raised the convertible top when we left the restaurant. The Chrysler had a bench-style front seat and I wanted to sit close to Danny, actually to snuggle up, but I didn't want to overplay my hand. I felt that I had, if not verbally, physically shown him my high card. Strangely, I wanted to get home, to Cossins, to familiar territory. I would not be more confident there, I knew, but more grounded. My confusion was growing and I thought perhaps that home would normalize, stabilize my relationship with Danny. After all, Cossins was where Danny had found Edie—and had lost Edie—but there, at least, it would be easier for me to regain my proper role in Danny's life which was, really, at least in Cossins, little role at all. I began to wonder about the reason and the justification for the two trips Danny and I had taken together. Was Danny going somewhere with all of this or was I playing second fiddle while he tried to figure out where to go without Edie. The closer I got to Danny emotionally, it seemed, the further away moved the possibility of getting closer physically. As they say in real estate I couldn't afford to get into a bidding war with my sister (If she were ever able again to see herself in that position).

I took a shower to warm up physically. I didn't need to warm up emotionally. And I didn't want to betray myself to Rose and John. I put on a pair of lounging pajamas and matching robe and found Danny and his parents in the living room with their first drink, the men talking about their days, Rose straightening Johnny's picture on the mantel. The men rose as I entered the room and Danny asked me what I wanted to drink, although by this time he knew that I knew that it would be wine, anything red but no drier than Burgundy. He headed for the kitchen as his mother asked him to bring more cheese and crackers.

The conversation shifted to our day, Danny's and mine. John looked at me to begin. I love men, don't get me wrong, and I've already said that John, Danny's dad, reminded me of my father. But if you are a woman you know, generally speaking, that the eyes of men are less likely to plumb your depths than those of a woman. I probably should not have been concerned about either of Danny's parents, they've treated me gloriously as a house guest and as Danny's friend and Edie's sister. But we were having drinks and even without them human connections are not all that difficult to discern. I had spent a lot of time with Rose but that, notwithstanding, I knew that she, not John, could and would like to, open me up with a mental scalpel to see in which ventricle, if either of my heart, her son was living. It didn't, as they say, get much tenser than that.

As I began with Buckingham Fountain and the Art Institute Danny came in with my wine and a plate of cheese and crackers. The cheese was yellow and looked soft and the wine was inviting. I said a silent prayer that it would not act as a scalpel and open my heart.

The conversation was fun. Everyone took part. John and Rose listened attentively and asked questions of both Danny and me with perhaps a few more directed to me as a stranger to the city. I didn't need to make anything up to convince Rose and John both that I was duly impressed with Chicago and that I could see why they loved it.

"Chicago," I said, to a question from John asking for a comparison between the city and Cossins. "Forgive me" I said, "but I was taught that comparisons are not productive and should be avoided if possible. But your question is a good one, so let me just say that, aside from the obvious differences in grandeur—the lake, the skyscrapers, the culture, the magnitude of it all—that I'd say that if Cossins is a local parish church Chicago is a cathedral. How would you compare Chicago to New York?"

Rose spoke first. "I've never been to New York," she said. "But John has, several times on business."

I was enjoying myself immensely. I love conversation. The room was warm and I think the wine and snacks actually made it warmer. I was already in love with Danny and I felt that Rose and John were two people I could love spending time with, especially in the company of Danny. The ball, so to speak, passed to John.

"That's a tough question, Liz," he said. "Chicago is the second largest city in population but third, after New York and Los Angeles, in area. New York and Chicago share more in common in appearance and in the culture of neighborhoods." John took a sip of what looked like his scotch and reached for a piece of cheese. I couldn't get over how much he reminded me of my dad. I felt as if it would take nothing for me to become part of this family. I could tell that Danny was enjoying a family scene that so comfortably included me. "I'm going to say something that I know won't offend anyone present but might somewhere else, like in a local tavern, and this is a major oversimplification. To use your own phrasing, Liz, if New York is a city Chicago is a town. Honey," he said to Rose, "don't hit me with the olive in your martini."

Rose laughed. "Very good, Dear," she said. "I don't disagree at all. And I wouldn't throw my giant, Italian, stuffed olive at anyone. I love them too much." She looked down at her glass on the side table and said, "Danny, Dear, would you get your mother a refill, please? I like your description, John. During the war most of the servicemen said that their favorite cities were Chicago and Philadelphia because they were big enough for fun and small enough for warmth. They said they liked the friendliness of the people. And that certainly fits Chicago. Many GIs riding the EL were invited home for dinner by someone they didn't even know. What's that line in Frank's song, 'My kind of town'? I guess that says it all."

Danny checked his watch. "I'm hungry, Mom. What's for dinner?"

Rose looked at her wrist. "My," she said, "looks like we're going to be fashionable tonight, dinner at eight. It's almost ready, Danny, and it's called Saturday night special: hamburgers, french fries, salad and beer. Better wash up."

I looked at Danny. He winked at me. Boys, I thought. Boys and their moms. And food. Things will never change.

The Saturday supper was Chicago-good stuff. Dinner talk ranged all over the place from Kennedy's assassination to the onset of the hippy sixties to the very recent appearance of the miniskirt. Appearing to be uninterested I thought, John reached for more salad and Danny snagged another hamburger. I'd let Rose measure her husband's reaction to this last topic but I thought I saw Danny trying too hard to act indifferent. Skirts, after all, and dresses are the really significant clothing separators between men and women. I'd heard Uncle Rich say to his girlfriend Blanche once that he'd never date a girl who didn't or wouldn't wear a skirt. Pants, he said, are alright on a ladder but even in golf they are completely unnecessary and distracting from the women's game. Women, Uncle Rich concluded, are the only things that separate men from the neanderthal club. Even the pictures and diaramas I'd seen that day at one of the museums showed the cave woman wearing a skirt. And now, it seemed, after being delivered from the Victorian Era, men had the gift of the miniskirt. When I made that observation Danny perked up and said, "Yes, but everything's a trade-off. We traded the hoopskirt for the mini while losing the cleavage."

"Now, Danny," Rose said. "Let's not embarrass Liz."

Suddenly there was a rare silence. "Don't mind me," I said, "I think the conversation is delightful. What woman wouldn't?"

John offered coffee. I said no thanks, that I was tired and needed some sleep. I offered to help Rose in the kitchen but she said no, that it was getting late and we all needed to retire. I hugged Danny and kissed him on the cheek, forgetting until too late that I was wearing pajamas and that my breasts were soft against his shoulder. This had been, to paraphrase another writer, a day to remember. As I lay my head on my pillow and closed my eyes it hit me again: Edie should be in this bed—or better, in Danny's bed. I knew that every day, every minute I spent with Danny was cementing it for me but I wanted to know so badly where Danny was. I knew I'd never ask. I was afraid even to think of it, afraid that I knew already.

The next morning, Sunday, at breakfast, Rose asked if I felt like going to church. As a Catholic I was a bit surprised by the question but then I knew that such topics were not usually comfortable.

"Yes," I said, "that would be nice," not knowing what was coming next as I wasn't sure where the Landy's religious affiliation lay.

"There are several Catholic churches nearby," Rose said. "We're Anglicans," she said, "if it's okay we'd love to have you come with us."

Ordinarily it would make a difference, I thought. But something, and of course I thought of Danny, of sitting next to him in church, made it easy for me to say, "I think I'd like that, going to your church."

"We have Holy Communion every Sunday," Rose said. "Actually every day. You're welcome to participate."

"I'd love to go," I said, "but I'd better just watch during communion, if you don't mind."

Rose smiled. "That's fine," she said, "we understand."

The Church of the Atonement was a few miles south of the apartment just off Sheridan Road. It was built of stone with lots of stained glass. It looked very Catholic. At once I felt comfortable but knew that receiving communion was out of the question, and I hoped that they really did understand. After Mass—that's what they actually called it—we greeted the priest—that's what they actually called him—and stood on the sidewalk next to the car.

"Liz," John said, "Rose and I would like to take you and Danny to lunch. One of our favorite places is called the Villa Venice. It's several miles north along the lake but the drive is beautiful and the food outstanding. I know you and Danny have to leave tonight but we'll have plenty of time to get things together before we leave for the airport. I took Danny's arm in the chill breeze off the lake and we piled into the back seat. I'd been anxious to get back to Cossins but now I wasn't sure. A weekend like this, I knew, might never happen again.

The Villa Venice was a large, almost sprawling place in what I would call a country setting. It was beautiful and possessed serenity one might expect from a manor house on an English moor. It most certainly was not an urban restaurant. It was not a place you just dropped in on. It was a place you had to drive to, a place you had to plan to go to. And that gave it the romantic mystique the owners were obviously striving for. Patron traffic was not of primary concern. Excellent food, high prices and ambience were. In the expansive garden stood an old, large, stone well. On the lip of the well rested a metal cup. Danny went over to it, picked it up, and dipped water from a wooden bucket. I went to him. Suddenly I was enveloped by the smell of what I could only describe as rotten eggs.

Danny chuckled and offered the cup to me. He said it was sulfur water. I wanted to be a good sport so I held my nose and took a small sip. It was very cold and the cold offset the smell. Danny said that when he was a child they would come here and he and his dad would taste the water but his mom and Johnny didn't like it. As we walked toward the restaurant John said to me, taking my arm, "Do you like Frank?"

Did I like Frank? Was the pope Catholic? Was World War II a tragedy? I'd yearned as a thirteen-year-old to go to Saint Louis or Chicago to see Frankie Boy and swoon with all the other thousands of girls as he looked into their eyes, made them feel that he was singing only to them, and crooned "All of Me" and every girl in the audience wanted to, wanted to take all of him, or so they thought. But we didn't have the money and Mom said it wouldn't seem right with Edie off in the Pacific on the *Mercy*, mending soldiers and sailors and getting shot at.

"I love Frank," I said.

"A friend of his owns this place," John said. "And when Frank's in town he always comes out here to do a few shows as a favor to his friend. You can't get in the place."

I felt warm on John's arm. I nudged closer to him. "I'd have found a way," I said, looking up at him. "You could have bet on that."

The waiters were all in black and white with white serving towels over an arm. The wine and the food were great. Danny and I shared a pate de foie gras before dinner and we both had porterhouse steaks. I was so busy I don't remember what Rose and John had. Before dinner John had a couple of what he called single malt scotches. Rose stuck with her martinis and Danny and I had dry vermouth cocktails—I told him the plane ride made me a bit woozy and I didn't want to help it along.

As seems to be always the case the ride home was subdued. Danny knew he had to go back to work but I knew he'd miss his mom and dad and they'd miss him, especially since there was no Johnny around to take up the slack. No matter how much fun you're having you know, job or not, that the time to leave always lurks. I looked forward to getting home, who doesn't? But I'd enjoyed meeting Rose and John and knew I'd miss them. Love is great but the payment always comes due.

THIRTEEN

THE FAULT, THE MISTAKE WAS mine and mine alone but it was six months later before I recognized it, and by then I was in Hollywood. I made the error on the plane on the way home from Chicago. It had been but a weekend, a long weekend but it seemed more like we had walked through a dream. Danny and I were on the plane to St. Louis in the cocoon that is every plane in flight. Side by side we sipped our drinks letting the magic of Chicago surround us like water in a swimming pool after a dive. Of course, we'd left John and Rose behind but, as I think must be typical, part of them flew with us, including part of Johnny who lived now on the mantel. I could smell Rose's perfume and feel the strength of John's arm as we walked from the fountain to the Villa Venice. How, I thought, is it possible for people you've known less than a week to enter your psych, penetrate your very being? Would it be possible to do for those who have no visceral connection to someone you loved. I luxuriated in the thought that when we got to Saint Louis we still had Danny's car, still had the ride home to Cossins, still had the luxury of sitting next to Danny while the heater worked in the cold to bring us closer together to allow me to dream, to wonder if, during that last leg of the trip I'd fall asleep on Danny's shoulder and he might kiss me on the lips or accidentally let his hand fall carelessly on my breast.

The mistake I'd made on the plane was an impulsive one and I was not known as an impulsive person. Maybe it was the second drink, the one in the air. I pulled a letter from my purse, a letter in an envelope with the sender's brand, so to speak, in the upper left hand corner, "Paramount Pictures Hollywood." No address, just a statement of power and understated glamour. Danny read the letter, I could tell, more than once. Without looking at me he took a sip of his drink and said, "Liz, are you going to California?" I thought his question conveyed more warmth than anything he had said or done since I fell in love with him. Immediately, although I knew we'd have to discuss California sooner or later, I felt I'd made a mistake. Was this unexpected moment, I thought, both the beginning and the end of what I'd wanted all along? I was not asleep on Danny's shoulder but he leaned over and kissed me, kissed me on the mouth. He smiled. "Of course you must go," he said. And then he said two more things that threw me for a loop: "I'll be here when you get back," he said. He smiled again. "They want to make a movie of your Rawlings novel. And if you don't like their lawyers I'll be glad to help out."

We were both tired. The ride to Cossins was quiet except for the twin hums of the engine and the heater. I didn't fall asleep on Danny's shoulder and he didn't kiss me again and his hands, both of them, stayed on the steering wheel. As in fiction, as in a short story especially, we'd just passed the climax of our story and were now in that slide toward the end known formally as the denouement. If I'd known then what I learned later, I would not have been on the proverbial cloud nine when Danny dropped me off at home and I might have worn a cotton nightgown that night instead of the only silk one I owned. I wanted silk dreams that night, not cotton, and I had them.

It was after dinner and, except for Dad and Edie the whole family was there. Mom had spread the news, the big news, the good news (we hoped) about Paramount and my novel about Marjorie Kinnan Rawlings, the great and my favorite writer. Uncle Rich and Blanche had come, too, and of course Cary, Mom's new husband. We'd had a celebratory dinner before, really, we had anything to celebrate except a faint promise of hope.

They say that good writers, real writers, write for themselves and that their work is enough reward. But, of course, every artist who is still rational wants to see at least someone else view and, if possible, enjoy and appreciate their efforts as well as their pleasure. Unless you're a screenwriter the first oracle of and to the writer is the publisher and, in Dorrance, my publisher, I had, I was sure, the best. This because, although I had no word nor proof of it, without Dorrance and their efforts on my behalf Paramount, let alone any of Hollywood, could not have known of my work.

Cary offered to buy my plane ticket. Danny said he'd put me up in a hotel. And Uncle Rich said he and Blanche would like to go with me, not they said of course, as chaperones but because they'd never been West. After just a few minutes Blanche's enthusiasm erupted and she said that Uncle Rich had asked her to marry him and she'd said yes only if they could, as she put it, "run over to Las Vegas and get married in one of those glitzy wedding chapels." Uncle Rich nodded, obviously feeling both exhilarated and victorious. There was Champagne and hugs and well-wishes all around and I began to feel like a celebrity before I'd ever left town.

Of course, Dad wasn't there, couldn't be. I remembered suggesting to Edie after she came home from the war that it might be a good idea to find an anchor for her life and that maybe it needn't be a person. She had found Jesus Christ in the convent and I had found my anchor in front of the Royal Mom had bought me. At that moment I prayed not only that we had both found our own treasure but that the discovery had been guided by the Lord. Mom seemed so happy: her precious girls, as she would put it, had both found their anchors. "God is good," as she was so fond of saying, and it sure looked that way to me, too. Funny, I thought, the two people I missed so much right now were both with the Lord, in their own way.

I needed some money to sustain myself in Hollywood for an unspecified period of time so I took Cary's offer of the plane ticket.

I didn't need Danny's offer of the hotel it turned out as Paramount would provide a cottage near the studios as a temporary residence and study area as I imagined I'd need for any work they assigned me on the script. The first thing I learned in that regard was that I was expected to understand that there would be changes to my book to accommodate its transmission to the screen. I signed that written waiver and at the bottom wrote my own: The film is yours, the book is mine. I sent a copy of the contract to Danny for his approval. Our separation was painful for me and, I hoped but wasn't sure, for him. I had a job to do, a really big job at least for me and, although I had a hard time feeling his love, even at home sometimes, let alone in California, I could feel his support. That kiss on the plane, on the mouth, was a big help and kept me going when I felt lonely and unworthy of what was going on at Paramount. Danny noted that the monetary compensation arrangement line in the contract was blank. Whatever your percentage is, he said, be sure it's of the gross and not the net. There could be no net in the long run after payrolls and other expenditures. Of course I tucked that advice away for future reference and hoped that it wouldn't be needed. I didn't know how long the process would take nor how long they'd need me around. I was prepared to stay, even to suffer if necessary, for as long as it took. After all I wasn't William Faulkner, a man who, I learned, had done more than a fair amount of Hollywood writing himself. I was deeply in love with Danny but I had to realize that it didn't pay much, at least not right now.

For the most part the people were nice to work with and I didn't need to dress up for work even though I couldn't get used to all the women in pants. I figured it was California or maybe just the studio but I stuck with my skirts and blouses. The women tried to make up for the pants with bullet-bras but I could see that that only invited more attention, wanted attention. A few of the men and the women were condescending. I assumed that was because I was a novice and not because of my age as I had long passed the starlet stage. After about a week I took a bus downtown and bought myself the cheapest wedding ring I could find. Danny had said that he'd be there when I got back. I trusted that but I didn't want any interference. I wanted Danny. Something did bother me, though. Again, maybe it was the palm trees and the Pacific Ocean but I began to think and worry less about Edie. I knew this wasn't good. At this point she was, as they say, "my main man," but my life had changed radically from Cossins and I had a lot to do and a lot on my mind. I prayed for her, especially knowing that her final vows were not too far away. And I tried hard not to kid myself. There's a song that starts, "Somebody else is taking my place . . ." How did the girlfriends and wives manage I wondered during the war while they waited at home with little hope and waning patience. If they met someone else they did so with pain but not without some understanding. I hoped that Edie didn't feel abandoned by me but she had chosen her new world. We were not nor never would be again girls in the same house often sharing the same bed and the same dreams. And I was still feeling the pea under my blanket, so to speak. After all I was in love with what amounted to her man had different choices been made. Letters from home helped to keep me going but I'd heard nothing from Edie. Maybe it was because I hadn't bothered to find out if letters were possible at this stage of her progress. Life does get kinda thorny, I thought. But then the King of the Universe didn't have it too easy either, did He?

FOURTEEN

"I HAD NO IDEA I'd be gone so long. I'm so glad to be home. Southern California is lovely, the weather impeccable. No wonder they decided to locate the movie studios there. The line between the make-believe and the reality of Los Angeles is so thin it's easy to see how the dramatists and the actors can walk back and forth across that line as if in and out of a fog and there's plenty of that, too. I missed you so. Of course, I missed Danny terribly but when I'm away from home—and home really means you, Mom—my heart travels here to this lovely house and all its memories."

We were sitting, just the two of us, Mom and me, at the kitchen table sipping tea. It was the first day of spring. The Lord and Lady cardinals were talking to each other, probably, I thought, about their second mating of the year and where she'll build their nest. He shares incubation chores with his wife and feeds the young of the first brood by himself while she builds the second nest. How sweet, I thought, how much we humans could learn by watching what we like to think of as the lesser species.

I had written in the morning, working on my World War II novel set in the Pacific and carefully avoiding stepping on my sister's toes with any of the characters.

The lunch dishes were done and put away. The afternoon sun rayed through the motes stirred by the kitchen activity and settled on our hands, mine still young and inexperienced, Mom's veined with the wisdom, the only real wisdom, of motherhood. It was beautiful. It was serene. It was too precious to smash but I did it anyway. I'd planned to do it. After all, one couldn't do it without planning. "Mom," I said, "I'm pregnant."

I know there are several ways to say that, even better ways, but Mom was not the fancy type and between two women, especially two women who wear the titles Mother and Daughter, no other way is needed. Had I said it to Dad he'd have understood the English of it but perhaps not the meaning of it, at least not the meaning that moved silently between Mom and me, between two females for only females can fully understand what those female organs do to the woman, for the woman. We were, Mom and I, sharing a world so much different, so much larger than our kitchen or our house or Cossins or even the whole of the state of Missouri that only a female Albert Einstein or Albert Schweitzer or Winston Churchill or Socrates could fathom it.

Mom took my hand, as I was sure mothers had done since the start of time. First she studied my hand and then read my eyes. Steady as a rock, betraying nothing of her feelings she said, "Go on, Liz." It was not just her way of telling me to continue, it was her way of letting me know that she was there, that she'd always be there for me, that nothing was wrong, that babies cannot ever be wrong.

"I think I made a big mistake, Mom," I said. "I told Danny in a letter that I'd bought a wedding ring because I didn't want to be bothered by would-be Romeos at the studio, not because of any recent experience or imminent fear but just because of stories I'd heard. You know how the distance of separation magnifies the imagination. Danny immediately wired me that he was flying out and I didn't have the time—or the will, really—to stop him. It had been several months and I missed him terribly. Actually, I felt good about seeing him and I probably would have done nothing to stop him if I could."

"And he flew out?" Mom said.

Mom still held my hand. "Yes. He had my address. He took a cab. Oh, Mom, it was so good to see him. He held me and for the first time we kissed mutually, together. For the first time I felt that maybe Danny loved me as much as I did him."

I had a small kitchenette in my cottage. He brought a bottle of chilled champagne and we celebrated together. I had a few things in the refrigerator but he insisted we go out to dinner. I don't remember the place but it was nice, you know, Hollywood style.

He took my hand, the left one, the one with the wedding ring on it. "I couldn't stand the thought of your being harassed by some Errol Flynn or lackey on the set, or even by a writer who thought he might help you more than you wanted."

After dinner we sat and talked about how they make a movie out of a book and about a couple of cases he was working on. The waiter brought more water and coffee. I was ready to go but Danny ordered two B&Bs. I felt a little sheepish about scaring him with the wedding ring but I was so excited to see him, to be with him. The restaurant had air conditioning. It was cool but the dinner and the drinks and Danny made me take off my sweater.

Suddenly he removed the wedding ring and kissed my hand, kissed the finger where the wedding ring had been. My eyes teared up. I stroked his cheek with my hand. We toasted with our pony glasses. He took a diamond ring from his jacket pocket. It was not in a box. He slipped it on my ring finger. "Liz," he said, "will you marry me?"

"Oh, Mom, I can't tell you how I felt," I said.

"I think I may know," she said. "And the diamond?"

I took the ring from my skirt pocket and slipped it on my finger. "Isn't it beautiful?" I said.

She took my hand. "It fits you perfectly," she said. She smiled. "Don't take it off again until you need to make room for the wedding ring."

I couldn't smile back at my mom. I started to cry. "But, Mom," I said. "What about Edie?"

Mom hugged me across the kitchen table. "Liz, Honey," she said, "I'm so happy for you both, you and Danny. I wish you a lifetime of the kind that your dad and I shared." Then she cried with me. She told me long ago that crying was good but not alone. "Have you asked Danny that question?" she said. "Have you asked Danny what about Edie?"

I thought for a moment. "No," I said. "I guess I thought, you know, the convent and all."

"Liz," she said, "your sister has not taken her final vows. It seems to me you have a job to do, a job that may well be more difficult than writing a book."

◈◈◈ ◈◈◈ ◈◈◈

I wore my engagement ring. At least one reader might want to ask why. I guess it's because somewhere along the way I either learned or convinced myself that what you don't tell now you will have to tell sooner or later.

We were seated in the living room after our traditional Holy Saturday meal. Lent was over so we had wine with dinner and brandy and coffee afterwards. Danny and I were seated on the couch facing the fireplace. Cary and Mom were in the two chairs flanking the fireplace, each now with its own side table. Edie sat alone in the chair to my right, Dad's chair, the big loungy one with the large matching ottoman. It was cool but Edie wore a pale yellow dress for Easter, her long, slim legs across the ottoman.

"Edie, Dear," Mom said, "there's plenty left in the kitchen if you're hungry."

We'd been caught off guard. Edie just came in almost as if she'd never been gone. So far no one had asked and she hadn't offered an explanation. Maybe she figured the answer to any question had to be more than obvious: she had not taken her final vows and, dressed as she was, had left the convent. It was also possible that one, she didn't want to talk about it for some reason and two, she felt that over the past few years enough had been learned through visits, letters, and phone calls that further discussion was unnecessary. Lastly, and I think we all acknowledged this silently, there might well have been an element of shame or at least embarrassment at what she saw as her failure in spite of the fact that her decision to leave the convent was exactly what the novitiate had been established for even centuries ago.

We'd had the usual baked ham and sweet potatoes and stuff. Edie said, "Thanks, Mom, but I've already eaten. I had dinner with Roger Sullivan at one of his daughter's homes. You may remember Roger, he's the chief administrator at the hospital. He was at Dad's funeral. Cary, you must remember him. You worked together for years."

Cary grinned. "Yes, Edie, I know Roger well and he's a great guy and a good father as far as I know. I like him."

Mom smiled and nodded, still sensitive I guessed at the thought of Dad. Danny and I really couldn't contribute anything so we just looked on in approbation. The atmosphere around my sister seemed to tighten and when Edie spoke next I understood why—or I thought I did. My first thought was that I was showing. I wore an overblouse and a loose skirt but even that could have been a tip-off; and of course there was the engagement ring, not to mention Danny on the couch beside me. But I was wrong on all three counts.

Although she was wrong she felt she couldn't look to Danny for support. And Cary was a spectator. So she looked at Mom with a bit of a tear in one eye and supplication in her voice. "Mom," she said, "Roger and I have started dating."

Of course I couldn't anticipate everyone's reaction, even my own really. At first a little cloud of confusion covered the living room. Danny squeezed my hand. Cary lighted another cigarette and took a sip of brandy. He was only fairly recently involved but, after all, he was Mom's husband. Mom stood up and went to Edie. She sat next to her on the ottoman and hugged her. They both started crying. It hadn't really been what Edie had said. Mom's daughter, my sister was home. We were taught that our lives didn't belong to us first. They belonged to God. But God gave us our choices and Edie had just revealed two of hers. At our level, at our family level, it was Edie's life, Edie's choices and she was home and right now that was all that mattered to the people in that room, the most important people in her life to which she had just added Roger. God was good and we all knew it, felt it down deep for our Edie.

Danny waited for his opportunity and went to Edie, the girl he'd once wanted to marry. He pulled her to her feet and hugged her tight. It made me feel so good I started to cry. Finally, Cary said, "Marie, is there another bottle of champagne in the fridge?

We need to celebrate." There was no mention of my ring nor of my almost too obvious condition and I was glad. This day belonged to Edie.

The End

December 19, 2012
6:51 A.M.
San Mateo, Florida

EPILOGUE

DANNY AND I WERE MARRIED after Easter on June 12, his mother's birthday. We were married by an Anglican priest in Danny's home parish in Chicago with a promise that after a year our priest at Saint Ambrose would have a blessing ceremony there. We returned home to Cossins with Rose and John for the reception and for everybody to get together and get acquainted. Rose Marie Landy was born on Thanksgiving Day of that year, 1966. Everyone is still arguing about whom she looks like but the prevailing view is a combination of, strangely enough, the two grandfathers, my dad, Roy, and Danny's dad, John. Of course, it doesn't really matter as she is the most beautiful girl in the world right now and there is no doubt, everyone agrees, that she will look nothing like either grandfather when she grows up except perhaps for her hair and eyes. Danny has been promoted to partner in his law firm and loves his work but can't wait to get home to Rose Marie and me and, of course, vice versa. I'm still at work on my WWII novel and the Rawlings film is due out in about six months. I had no idea it took so long to make and market a movie. Of course, Mom and Cary are delighted to have Rose Marie and Danny and me staying at the old homestead and we are happy to be there but if another child comes along we have plans to get our own place somewhere in town, somewhere not too far away from

Mom and Cary. And we already have scheduled regular trips to Chicago to see Rose and John and to introduce Rose Marie to Lincoln Park and the beauties and wonders of Chicago and to the places where her father played and grew up. Uncle Rich and wife Blanche moved to California. I think it had something to do with their visit when I was out there. He is teaching at Pepperdine and Blanche is working as an assistant librarian. As Mom likes to say, God is good.

Edie and Roger are living in his home after their wedding in the hospital chapel. His daughters are scattered about and doing well. None of them is married yet but if looks has anything to do with it it won't be long before the bells ring, as they say. The state built a new wing on the hospital partially designed to welcome returning vets from both the big war and the Korean War who have been experiencing problems adjusting to civilian life and those with accompanying physical problems. Edie's husband, Roger, asked her to direct this unit citing her medical experiences and ability to identify with both male and female GIs at their level. Edie says that, and not strangely, her time in the convent has helped her to cope with her phobia. She says that coming to know Jesus so intimately both as a God and as a man has given her the strength to move on. And, of course, Roger as her husband and Cary as a potential counselor are comforting and nearby. Regarding children she cites her age, forty-two, as an indication that the clock is ticking. She mentioned adoption as a possibility but personally I see Edie and Roger as dedicated professionals and lovers. She says that the memories of the *Mercy* are good but fading and those of the Japanese prison can still frighten her to a stiff, sitting position in the middle of the night. Roger, she says, is both gentle and understanding. Of course, this is Edie's story but without the love of all the rest of us it might have been much shorter.

❖❖❖ ❖❖❖ ❖❖❖

The following summer, that of 1967, Mom called Mr. Branam, the manager of the Edgewater Beach Cottages at Lake of the Ozarks to reserve a week at Chateau-Thierry. She said there would be six of us, though, and it might be crowded. He said he had a few new sofa beds in storage that would fit nicely in our cabin and that he would place one there before we arrived as well as giving the place a good cleaning, as usual. Mom and Cary would have one bedroom, Roger and Edie the other and, since Danny and I had the baby and would need the bathroom during the night, the sofa bed. It would be a tight week but we were now all family and when the week was over we'd be more so.

It was wonderful. Mr. Branam saw to it that we had extra Adirondack chairs out front; we couldn't all fit on the little front porch. Mom confessed to me later that she had thought of renting one of the larger units, concerned about memories of Dad. But, reverting as we all seem to do to the thought if not the dream that our loved ones who had died might somehow join us from a heavenly perch, and since Dad had both fought at and named the cottage Chateau-Thierry, she decided that Dad would rather join us there than at some place he didn't know. As usual, Mom was right. I didn't ask Edie, but I felt Dad's presence and it meant a lot to me. It was a great time. Little Rose Marie played in the shallow water by the shore. The rest hung out on the platform, took naps, or, to get out of the sun for awhile, drank a beer on the cottage porch. We intended as much relaxation as possible and that included as little cooking and dishwashing as we could manage. Determined to avoid the hassle of restaurants Roger and Edie hopped into their car (It was no longer Edie's green Olds sedan) and made regular trips to the local deli in town and came back with all kinds of goodies in paper and plastic just right for the garbage can that waited like a faithful servant whose duty it was to save us from the kitchen sink.

At night there were stories around the circle of chairs in the yard with after-dinner drinks as the unbeatable Missouri sunset painted the lake in oranges and reds and blues. We learned a lot about each other and ourselves that we might not have learned in any other way or setting. We talked about family that none of us knew about. We talked about the wars that had taken some of ours from us. I teared with Rose when

Johnny's name came up and with Mom as she described the battle of Chateau-Thierry as she'd heard it from Dad.

The stories were wonderful and sad and they worked to meld us and weld us into one newer and larger family. We reinforced what we already knew: that the family is the nugget, the golden nugget of society, of the world.

ACKNOWLEDGEMENTS

EDITH BEARDSLEY, MY MOM AND first English teacher; Patricia Martin, my inspiration and love; Mary Might, my editor and manuscript preparer; Mary Daniels, my daughter and inspiration; All the great people at iUniverse Publishing who made this book possible.